The Last Swordmage
Volume 1 of the Swordmage Trilogy

By
Martin F. Hengst

A Magic of Solendrea Novel

Nathan -
It was great working with
you. Keep following your interests. best
of luck in the future.

Warmest Regards,

30-AUG-2013

DEDICATION

This book is lovingly dedicated to my father, whose passion for reading inspired me to create my own fantastic worlds and all the wonders that exist within them.

OTHER TITLES IN
THE SOLENDREA SERIES

TABLE OF CONTENTS

Chapter 1

Winter had come to the Frozen Frontier and with it, hunger and desperation. The autumn harvest had been meager, marred by drought and constant incursions by rival clans.

Salt was the primary ingredient in any meal of late, Tiadaria thought bitterly. Salted beef and salted fish had become all too common. At least the salt made it harder to taste the less than palatable side dishes that accompanied the main meal. Her stomach rumbled in protest, loudly reminding her that portion sizes had suffered as much as the quality. The men and boys ate first. Whatever was left was split among the women and girls. This was the way of the clan.

She shifted the yoke across her shoulders, careful not to splash any water out of the buckets that hung on each end of the curved pole. She glanced up and down the field. There was no one else about. The men had gone hunting and the majority of the women and children were gathered together in the long house, weaving rushes into mats. The rough mats were uncomfortable, but at least it was better than sleeping on the frigid ground. Tiadaria sighed and with a last survey of the area, tugged the rope loop from the gate and slipped inside, closing it behind her.

Her father had scolded her time and again for cutting through the paddock instead of going around. It spooked the animals and made them harder to feed and milk, he'd said. The aurochs never seemed to mind her presence, lowing to her in their mournful voice whether she passed through the paddock or not.

Still, he was the Folkledre of her clan and she suspected that his loud, often public, berating of her shortcomings served to reinforce his claim of impartiality when it came to clan business. Tiadaria received no preferential treatment. Regardless of being the Folkledre's daughter, she was still a girl, and therefore less important than even the babes who had been blessed with the good fortune to be born male.

Approaching the far end of the paddock, Tiadaria saw that she had picked the worst possible day to defy her father. He stood at the gate, his expression black. Another man stood beside the Folkledre. He was only about as tall as Tiadaria, but he was wrapped in so many sleek furs that he looked more like a miniature bear than a man.

A wagon was parked not too far off, with a long string of pack animals spread out behind it. They pulled at their tethers, obviously unhappy to be stuck in a place with nothing to graze on but ice and snow. The horses that drew the wagon were the finest beasts that Tia had ever seen. Their manes were long and silky, their coats lustrous under the winter sun. These horses made those that the clan owned look absolutely shabby in comparison.

When she reached the gate, her father swung it open. She passed through without a word. She was familiar with the expression he wore and had often born the bruises that had resulted from it. Silence was the better option. Tiadaria would speak when spoken to, and only when spoken to. Then, maybe, she would be able to spare herself the full fire of his wrath.

"Put those down, girl," the smaller man said. His voice put Tia in mind of a squealing piglet, high pitched, nasal and grating. "Let me get a look at you."

She looked to the Folkledre, not as the head of her clan, but as her father, seeking some comfort or reassurance there and finding none. He nodded curtly and motioned for her to deposit the yoke and its burden beside the paddock fence. As she bent to relieve herself of the load, she felt the little man's hand on her rump. Tia jerked upright, stepping away from his grasping hand even as she spun on her heel, her arm outstretched.

The Folkledre caught her wrist in a grip as cold and tight as a vice. Tia's stomach turned over. The sudden assault from two different fronts was making her ill. Her father had never been warm to her, true, but she had always attributed that to his station and responsibilities. She was a mere girl, but was it really possible that she meant nothing to him at all?

"She has spirit," the little man laughed. "What about my other terms?"

"She is clean and pure," the Folkledre replied, speaking for the first time. His voice was cold and harsh, like the wind that blew along the paddock fence. "You have my word, Cerrin."

"Surely you don't expect me to take you at your word?" The little man's eyes widened, feigning surprise. "Would you take me at mine?"

The clansman didn't reply. His hand still around Tia's wrist, he pulled her to stand in front of the swarthy little man. The Folkledre pulled her arm up behind her back, his other hand grasping her shoulder firmly.

Between the pain and the betrayal, Tiadaria panicked. She tried to strike out at her father with her free hand, and finding no way in which she could reach him, batted ineffectually at the man standing before her. Cerrin laughed and slapped her hand away. The grip on her shoulder intensified and the arm her father held behind her back was wrenched up so forcefully that she thought it would break.

"Stand still," the Folkledre snarled in her ear. "You dishonor the clan with your foolishness."

Stepping forward, Cerrin kicked her legs apart and grabbed the front of her breeches with one hand. Tia tried to scream, but all that came out was a hoarse croak. It dishonored the clan to try to fight for her own honor? Tears of anger, fear, and shame spilled from the corners of her eyes.

The slaver's free hand slid down her belly, like a cold snake, his thick fingers probing at the crease between her legs. She closed her eyes, begging to all the Gods she knew to either let her die, or wake her up from this horrific nightmare she had stumbled into. Please, she pleaded silently, please just let this be over. Her sobbing had become uncontrollable, a ragged gasping that made her tremble from head to foot. Cerrin's finger pressed deeper inside her, stopping as it met the resistance of her maidenhead.

Cerrin nodded, a broad smile spreading across his feral face. Her father released his grip on her, casting her unceremoniously aside. Tiadaria collapsed to the frozen ground, unable to stand, unable to do anything but cry and shake like the last autumnal leaf on a storm-ravaged tree.

"Your offer is acceptable, Folkledre." Cerrin said, taking a small wooden chest from the back of the wagon. He produced a thin metal band, a circlet the color of storm clouds with a thin wedge cut out of it. With the band in one hand, and an ominous looking black tool in the other, he knelt beside Tiadaria.

The fight had gone out of her. The violation had left her cold. Colder than the chill of winter in her barren, frost covered homeland. She felt as if she was observing herself from high above; a snow hawk on the wing looking down on her torment. Tia saw him fit the metal band around her neck and place the ends into the tool he carried. As he squeezed the device, a searing pain shot into the back of her neck and spread down her spine, branching out until it felt as if she had been plunged into the red hot fury of a forge's fire.

Tiadaria screamed, a raw, primal sound that tore at her throat and added to the agony coursing through her body. Just as she thought she wouldn't be able to endure any more, the pain was suddenly gone. Her entire body tingled, a lingering after effect of the systemic shock. She lay there, whimpering, on the ground, her fingers twitching spasmodically. When Cerrin slipped a pair of steel shackles around her wrists and locked them tight, she offered no resistance or even any indication that she was aware of his actions.

Later, Tiadaria would remember the minutest details. The clink of the coins landing in her father's palm; the words they exchanged as her father selected the two finest aurochs Cerrin had in his train; the wave of dread and despair that made the gorge rise in the back of her throat and the sudden, unavoidable knowledge that she had been sold into slavery by her own father. At the moment, however, she could only feel the tracks of her tears freezing in the bitterly cold winter morning.

Tiadaria's staring eyes reached the door to the long house, across the common square from the wagon and from where she lay shivering on the ground. Her mother stood in the doorway, her face expressionless, and her eyes blank pools of darkness. She turned and disappeared from view. No sign that she had witnessed what had just happened to her daughter, or cared.

Cerrin lifted her up. He was surprisingly strong for such a tiny man. He swung open the metal-braced door at the back of the wagon and shoved her through, into darkness. The door slammed behind her and Tia heard a clink of metal, the creaking of wood, and then the crack of a whip. The wagon lurched forward, bumping over the uneven ground.

Pushing herself upright, Tiadaria saw that she wasn't alone. A single candle burned in a lantern at the front of the wagon. Its pale, wavering light shone on two rough benches, separated by a much worn table. Four other girls were seated on the benches, two to a side.

Each of them were collared and shackled as she was. Tia, stood, wanting to sit on the bench rather than stay sprawled on the floor. As she got to her feet, the wagon hit a particularly deep rut and she was thrown forward. She careened off the edge of the table and into the girls on the opposite bench. A girl with long dark hair and oval eyes pushed her hard, slamming her back into the wall of the wagon. Tia slid down to the floor, her eyes watering from the unexpected assault.

"What's your name?" A petite blond on the end of the nearest bench asked quietly.

The girl with the dark hair kicked her under the table, slamming the toe of her thin boot into the other girl's shin.

"Shut your whore mouth, Darcy."

Darcy bowed her head and the dark-haired girl glared at Tiadaria.

"I'm in charge here, new girl. You'll do what I say, when I say. Got it?"

Tiadaria remained silent. She had had enough experience with her father's volatile temper and her brothers' harsh treatment to know that sometimes no answer was the best answer. She rapidly discovered that ignoring the problem wouldn't make her go away however, as the dark-haired girl stood up, grinding her heel into Tiadaria's boot.

"Come on, girls," the leader said with quiet malice. "Let's welcome the fresh meat."

The others fell on her, pinning Tia to the floor of the wagon. They punched her, slapped her, and pulled her hair. She tried to fight back, but the three of them held her down. They stripped off her boots and over tunic, tearing ragged holes in her breeches and blouse. They crowed with delight as purplish marks began to mar her fair skin where they struck her over and over again with clenched fists and the broad side of the shackles they wore.

Every girl in the wagon had a shot at her, all except Darcy, who huddled on the end of the bench and wept. When they were done with her, she was a bleeding, bruised mass crouched near the door to the wagon. The pain and shock had driven everything else out of her mind. Everything seemed gray and lifeless.

The passage of time meant nothing to her. They could have traveled an hour or a day and it wouldn't have mattered. Even when the wagon ground to a stop and Cerrin dragged her out by her hair, she hardly felt it. She was pushed roughly into a small room, the other girls thrown in behind her. The only sound that seemed to penetrate the fog surrounding her was the thud of a bar being dropped into place on the other side of the door. Never before had Tia felt so trapped and so very alone. She felt tears welling up and forced them back. She'd show no sign of weakness.

Darcy skittered to the corner of the room like a surprised insect and curled into a ball, hugging her knees to her chest. She looked as haunted as Tia felt. Tia wanted to go to the girl, the only one who had shown her any kindness. Darcy seemed safe. Tia wanted that limited comfort and to find out what she knew. She wanted to know what would happen to them, but the dark-haired girl stood in the middle of the room, swinging the chain between her shackled wrists in a menacing circle.

Without any warning or provocation, she darted to Tiadaria and kicked her hard in the ribs. From some distance, Tiadaria heard herself scream. The pain in her side was like nothing she had ever experienced. The girl kicked her again and again, and finally Tiadaria could bear it no longer. She retched, vomiting a thin froth onto the straw-covered floor. At least she was lucky enough that she had had nothing other than a bit of gruel that morning. The act of throwing up made her chest burn twice as badly.

Her tormentor laughed loudly, encouraging the other girls to come and see what she had done and join in. Darcy wasn't the only one to abstain this time. The fight seemed to have gone out of them. While they weren't curled up like Darcy, they looked away from the girl who was trying to egg them on. When she realized that her former co-conspirators were unwilling to rise to the occasion, she spit at them, and instead bent to grab Tiadaria by the hair.

"Filthy little whore, aren't you?" Steering her with a handful of hair, the girl forced Tia's face into her own vomit. "Lick it up. All of it."

Tiadaria managed to turn her head, which earned her a punch in the back of the skull. Lights flashed and her vision swam. She was suddenly very sure she was going to die. Please just let it end quickly, she begged no one in particular. Let me sleep and never wake up.

The dark-haired girl raised her hands to strike again and Darcy shot off of the wall as if she had been fired from a cannon. Her legs propelled her forward with such speed that, for a moment, Tiadaria thought she was in two places at once. Darcy lowered her head and shoulders like a bull and slammed into the tormentor's stomach. Her momentum carried the two of them to the far wall. They crashed into it together and then Darcy was atop the other girl, her eyes burning with murderous rage.

Darcy brought her hands together and slammed her wrists into the other girl's face. There was a sickening crunch, and blood sprayed across Darcy's face. There was a thin wail from the dark-haired girl that abruptly turned into a choking gurgle as Darcy brought the shackles down again and again. By the fifth blow, even the gurgle had stopped, but still the little blond girl continued her savage, animalistic attack. To

Tiadaria, the entire thing happened skewed to one side. She couldn't move, or even raise her head to gain the proper perspective.

Finally, the girl seemed to come to her senses. She sat astride her victim, blood, bits of hair and flesh clinging to the chain between her shackles. The other girls had cowered in the far corner of the room, clinging to each other in shock and terror. All the color had gone out of them and deep inside her, Tiadaria sympathized. The part of her that was nearer to the surface, however, rejoiced in Darcy's savage revenge. Tiadaria's only regret was that she hadn't been able to be a part of it.

On the periphery of her senses, Tiadaria was aware of shouting from outside the door. Her eyes were fixed on the blood that was slowly soaking the straw under the dark-haired girl's head. She heard the bar being lifted from the door and tried to lift her head but found she couldn't. Tia wondered, without much real concern, if the girl had left her paralyzed, unable to move for the rest of her life. She found that she could wiggle her toes in her thin boots and was reassured, just a little.

Hysteria and her sense of the absurd suddenly clashed together. Here she was, laying in a pool of her own vomit, a dead girl bleeding onto the floor not ten feet away, and she was thrilled that she could wiggle her toes. A thin rail of laughter burst out of her and the girls huddled together in the corner started to scream.

The door burst open and Cerrin dashed in, two other men on his heels.

"What the hell--" The slaver's outburst was cut short as he caught site of Darcy, who still hadn't moved from her place straddling what was left of the dark haired girl. She looked up at Cerrin and smiled. Her smile sent an ice cold shiver up Tiadaria's spine.

Whatever was inside that girl, it was no longer human. It looked up at them with no more reason or remorse than a wild animal. She just sat there, covered in blood, staring and smiling, smiling and staring. The slaver backed away, taking up a position near the door. His eyes darted from the girls in the corner to the murderous creature in front of him. He seemed not to notice Tiadaria for a long time. When he did, he swore under his breath. He turned to one of the men who had entered with him.

"Get her out of here, into another cell...and get a cleric. If she dies, I'm out twenty crowns and two prize beasts."

The man grabbed Tiadaria by the chain between her shackles and began to drag her across the floor to the door. Before he had pulled her into the hallway, she heard Cerrin speak again.

"Leave those two here. Move that one into another cell...and do something with the dead meat. There's a river down in the valley. We don't need the landlord asking too many questions. I've lost enough crowns today already."

Tia passed out, succumbing to the welcome blackness.

~~~~

Chapter 2

There was a knock at the door and Royce looked up from the pile of parchment he was working his way through. It was the Magistrate, a man who looked far too much like a weasel for the Constable's peace of mind. He stood in the doorway, a rat in men's clothes, his robes blocking out most of the sun that streamed in behind him.

"Constable," the Magistrate droned in his bee-like voice. Royce ground his teeth. "The executioner is ready to begin."

Royce flicked his hand and dropped his eyes to the parchment before him. "So let him begin."

The Magistrate sighed, a drawn out sound of long-suffering.

"Your presence is required, Constable. The executions cannot begin until you have taken your customary place on the platform."

Royce would have loved nothing better at that moment than to tell the Magistrate exactly where he could shove his custom and what he could do with it. when he got it positioned there. He sighed. Still, the man wasn't wrong. It was the customary duty of the Constable to attend every execution to see that every aspect of the king's law was followed to the letter.

He dropped the parchment and scrubbed at his face with the palms of his hands. Why, oh why, had he retired from the army and come to live in this tiny little town of absolutely no consequence, in the middle of nowhere? Furthermore, how was it that his little hamlet had managed to produce not one, but two criminals worthy of execution?

To be fair, he hadn't even looked at the death warrants. Royce had simply counter-signed the documents below the Magistrate's signature and filed them in the pile to be sent on to the capital. He supposed that he should take more pride in his work, but he was so tired of taking pride in anything. The entire reason he had picked this particular posting, out of all those that the King had offered him, was that it was sparsely populated and people would leave him alone. That way he could continue dying, slowly, in peace. In theory, at least.

"Fine," Royce finally acquiesced with a sigh. "I'll be there momentarily. Please go and let the executioner know that we will be proceeding as planned."

"As you command, Constable." The Magistrate accorded him a half-bow and withdrew, leaving the door standing open. One day that man was going to get his comeuppance, Royce thought bitterly. He only hoped that he was still around to see it when the happy day came to fruition.

Standing brought a fit of coughing that shook his fighter's frame. In a few moments, the fit subsided. The taste of copper was thick in the back of his throat. He took a vial from his belt pouch and swigged it down, grimacing at the vile taste. He wiped his mouth with his handkerchief, the cloth coming away from his lips tinged pinker than he would have liked.

His vigor drained, Royce walked out on the wide porch that surrounded the tiny, single room office. He pulled the door shut behind him and walked slowly toward the square and the throng of people who had congregated there. He was in no mood to deal with this nonsense today. Best to get it over with, and quickly.

The executioner was already on the platform, a hulking vulture of a man with the wardrobe to match. He was clad head to toe in the traditional black sackcloth vestments of his trade. His instrument, a wicked ax with a blade as long as Royce's arm, was slung over his shoulder, gleaming in the morning sun.

As Royce climbed the short steps, he was struck by how surreal the scene before him was. Normally the prisoners brought before the blade were the type of ruffian one would expect: murderers, thieves, rapists and the like. The girl that stood on the platform between two heavily armed guards couldn't have possibly been a threat to anyone.

Five feet tall if she was an inch, she was a mousy little thing, unsteady on her feet and swaying from side to side. Royce wondered if she might not be entirely in control of her faculties. She stood facing execution and yet seemed not to have a care in the world. She stared off into space, her eyes glazed, and her fingers twitching along to the songbirds nesting in the trees at the edge of the village.

If Royce had been pressed to pick the person least likely to be slated for execution out of the crowd, this girl would have easily made the top of the list. Something was wrong here. Perhaps he should have paid closer attention to the death warrants that crossed his desk. The crowd fell to a murmured hush as the Constable crossed the platform to his customary position near the Magistrate.

"What's the meaning of this, Magistrate?"

"The meaning of what, Constable?" The Magistrate withdrew his spider-like hands from the folds of his robe just long enough to motion for the executions to proceed.

"You know damn well the meaning of what," Royce seethed. "If that girl is a day over fourteen, I'll turn into a dragon and fly away."

The Magistrate spared him a sidelong glance before his eyes returned to the executioner, who was fitting the little blond girl with a hood.

"I wasn't aware that age had any bearing on the ability to commit a crime, Constable. You signed the death warrants yourself. Surely you don't dispute their validity now?"

"I don't give a lead crown over validity," Royce snapped. "What did this girl do to end up with her neck on the block?"

Finally the Magistrate turned, according the old soldier with his full gaze. His large watery eyes were full of contempt.

"She murdered another girl in cold blood. Are you going to argue that murder is no longer an offense that carries the penalty of death?"

Royce tugged at his lower lip. The executioner raised his blade.

"Wait!"

It was the right of the king's law for the Constable to commute any sentence, even death, but it was rare enough that only a handful of the elder folk in the crowd could remember such an occurrence. Royce had never nullified a sentence. Most of the people who ended up on the platform deserved it. With this one, he wasn't so sure. Maybe his curiosity was getting the better of him, but there was something here. Something he could feel at the back of his neck and the base of his spine.

He approached the girl and raised the hood from her head. It was then that he noticed the witchmetal collar around her neck. He sighed. She was a slave. That changed things. The girl's eyes seemed to look through him. He snapped his fingers in front of her nose until her lazy gaze met his.

"What's your name, girl?"

"Darcy," she said in a sing-song voice that sent a chill up Royce's spine.

"Did you kill a girl, Darcy?"

The little blond girl smiled a smile so wide and white that it put Royce in mind of the predatory fish that sometimes washed up on the shore at Blackbeach.

"Oh, yes. I killed her dead. I beat her down until she bled. In the head! Now she's dead." The girl cackled. "Dead! Bled! Dead! Bled!"

Royce shook his head and dropped the hood back over her head. He nodded soberly to the executioner and retreated to his station. The blade man pressed the girl's head to the block and an instant later, the crowd roared with approval. The executioner kicked the body off the platform, into a straw-filled cart parked below. Royce felt sick.

"Justice is done," the Magistrate remarked.

The Constable remained silent.

The village crier called for the next condemned and there was a commotion at the foot of the steps leading to the platform. There was a girl in chains, desperately fighting against the guards who struggled to keep her in place. Though she was shackled at wrist and ankle, she still fought, trying to tear the weapons from the belts of the men-at-arms attending her.

As the guards tried to march her up the short stairs, the girl went to ground, falling so quickly that the men had little time to react. When she hit the ground, she scrambled away as quickly as her bindings would allow. She was quick, but not quick enough. One of the guards ran her down and taking a blackjack from a belt loop, thwacked her soundly in the back of the head. The girl went limp, face down in the dirt. They lifted her under the arms and dragged her up the steps onto the platform, her feet dangling between them. They dumped her at the executioner's feet.

Royce watched as the ax man lifted the girl's body and placed her head in the block. The blow to the back of the head had knocked her senseless. Though her eyes were open, she was staring at some point far across a distant horizon. She also wore a witchmetal collar, its thin gray band a stark contrast against her pale skin. Her eyes were a deep, clear blue; the color of sapphire. Hair the color of corn flax dropped to her shoulders in a tangled mass. There had obviously been neither comb, nor brush, nor looking glass in whatever dank hole she had been assigned to for the night before her date with the sharp end of the blade.

She was definitely pretty, for a slave. Her nose was straight and unbroken, her eyes not sunken by years of abuse and neglect. She was newly collared then. A slave's life was notoriously hard and short, no matter how pretty they were. In fact, sometimes being pretty made it worse. There were those who would pay a premium for the chance to break such a lovely creature.

This one's high cheekbones and thick frame placed her in the far north before her capture. The Frozen Frontier, or very near, unless Royce missed his guess. He didn't. He was rarely wrong. There was something about her that piqued his curiosity. Something he couldn't quite place his finger on. There was a resonance about her, something that made the hair on his arms stand on end.

The girl had roused enough to start to struggle again. Rather than suffer through a repeat of her games with the guards, the executioner locked her shackles to the block, rendering her thrashing mostly ineffective.

Royce went rigid as the executioner offered the girl a hood, which she declined in a spate of colorful curses and epithets. She turned her head as far as the block would allow and attempted to spit at the blade man.

"Don't," the Magistrate said quietly. "This one deserves it too, just as the last one did."

The old soldier wasn't so sure. He watched as the girl tried to spit at the executioner a second time. It was a futile gesture, but enough to earn her a backhanded slap across her high cheekbones with a thick leather gauntlet. The executioner put his boot between her shoulder blades, pressing her neck into the edge of the block. The ax gave a dull ring as it was drawn across the platform and lifted to his shoulder.

The executioner hefted the blade and Royce found himself riveted. Most people closed their eyes in that final moment, or opted for the hood. She didn't. She kept her eyes open and fixed on the platform mere inches beyond her nose. The ax man's arms tensed for the swing and Royce sprang forward, landing on the balls of his feet. His hand flashed out, arresting the ax mid-stroke.

"Hold your blade," he said quietly but firmly. The crowd groaned. They were growing tired of the interruptions in their entertainment. Two executions and both stopped at the penultimate moment. Their dissension spread like wildfire through those who had assembled.

A swarthy little man with a bulbous red nose waddled onto the platform, his face suffused purple with rage.

"Enough! What's the meaning of this? She needs to die, and die now! She's filth. Vermin. A pestilence to be destroyed."

Royce eyed him up, studying the fine cut of the tunic, the flash of the large gems on each finger, the full purse tucked into his belt, the neck twisted and folded over to ensure that no coin could find its way out until it was called upon. He didn't know the man, but he knew the type. Royce raised an eyebrow and the ghost of a smile tugged at the corner of his mouth.

"Who are you, tiny creature, to question the Constable, former Knight of the Flame and Sergeant-at-Arms to the One True King?"

Rocking back on his heels, the man seemed to deflate, his face going from rage to confusion, to fear. He was obviously used to barking orders and expecting them to be followed without challenge. Probably backed by the bite of a whip. Slavers. Royce snorted derisively. They were all the same.

"My name is Cerrin, Mi'lord. I am a purveyor of...resources, foreign and domestic."

"What did this vermin do to have her neck placed on the block, slaver?"

The tips of the man's ears went red and he stammered a moment. He snapped his mouth shut and swallowed convulsively, then seemed to find his backbone.

"She's a menace. She attacked one of the other girls without provocation. Killed her in cold blood that one did. She cost me good crowns and I'll see to it that the others learn their place." The girl's spine went rigid as she fought against the restraints that held her down. It wasn't hard for Royce to believe that she had killed another slave. She fought like a caged animal.

"I didn't kill anyone, you filthy lying pig!" Spittle flew from her lips as the girl screamed at the little man. "Darcy was only defending me and you know it!"

"Do you dispute her claim?" Royce asked, almost conversationally. He fixed such a piercing gaze on the slaver that Cerrin went white.

"Err, no. Not exactly, Mi'lord."

"So she didn't kill directly? She was merely the cause of the, ah, altercation?"

"Yes. Yes! That's it precisely, Mi'lord." A smile flickered across the slaver's face. "She was an accomplice!"

Royce dropped his hand from the executioner's ax and waved him away. He knelt beside the girl and flipped up her thin shift, exposing the pale skin of her back all the way up to her breast band. Her sides were mottled in the green, purple, and yellow of aging bruises. It was an old slaver trick. Keep them in line, but only where the paying customers can't see. He ran a calloused hand down her side and the girl shied away from the touch. There were new layers of bruises on top of old here. There was no telling how long she had been brutalized this way.

"So she's to lose her head," Royce remarked quietly. "As an example for the others."

Royce jerked his head at the other girls, chained wrist to wrist, each with a thin witchmetal collar, clustered at the edge of the square.

The slaver had brought them here to teach them the consequences of rebellion. It was an age-old trick. Kill the usurper and keep the rest of the subjects in line. It was a trick Royce had used himself from time to time.

The slaver shifted from one foot to the other. Royce expected that he knew a trap when he walked into one, but he had offered the girl little mercy. He should expect none himself.

"So she dies as an example, the others fall in line." Royce was stalling now and he couldn't fathom why.

"Y-yes, Mi'lord."

Royce nodded, scratching his gray-black beard with gnarled fingers.

"How much," he asked after a long pause.

"Mi'lord?"

"How much did you pay for her? Surely she must have been quite a nuisance for you to waste perfectly good coin on executing her as an example. You could have done it with your own blade for free. But, then I don't suppose you like getting your hands bloody. So I ask you again, how much did you pay?"

The slaver's eyes darted from Royce to the girl and back again. The trap was sprung, he knew. Now all that was left was to see how much of his leg he'd have to lose to get free.

"Twenty crowns, Mi'lord. And a pair of aurochs."

Royce raised an eyebrow. "That's no small sum."

"Well, sir, she is untouched," the man blurted, then snapped his jaws shut as if he could cut the words off before they slipped out. He knew he had said too much.

"Ah." It was a softly spoken syllable, almost a sigh. Royce looked from the slaver down to the girl. He knelt and with a gentle touch, flipped her shift down to hide the bruises. "So you were looking to sell her to a man, then. One with, shall we say, peculiar tastes. Surely you'd have gotten top crown for her once she was fully functional."

"Not worth it," Cerrin sneered. "She's worth more to me minus her head."

Royce stood, his hand dropping to his belt. It hovered there a moment, poised over the foot-long dagger that was sheathed there. Beads of sweat stood out across the slaver's brow. He licked his lips in a constant nervous motion, his eyes watching Royce's hand and the blade hilt for any movement.

"You've no right," the Magistrate interrupted, stepping forward. Royce merely looked at him. The Magistrate withered under his glare. "Fine, do as you will." He threw his hands up and stormed off the platform, his robes swirling around his ankles.

Slowly, Royce dropped his hand to his purse and tugged it free. He unthreaded the lace and shook some coins into his hand, dropping the first few back into the pouch and palming the larger, thicker gold coins that sparkled in the muted morning sun. Each bore an underscored numeral twenty on the face and the namesake crown of the king on the reverse.

"Twenty crowns and two aurochs. I should think that forty crowns should cover your expenses and your, ah, inconvenience." Royce tossed the coins at the slaver's feet. They struck the platform and bounced with a dull ring, spinning for a moment before falling flat.

The slaver made no move to retrieve the coins. He stood there, still shifting from one foot to the other, his eyes flicking between Royce, the coins, and the girl. Royce tucked his purse back into his belt and tugged the loop from the hilt of his knife, laying his hand on the cap.

"You've made your sale, slaver. Take your payment, and go. Now."

A sudden cry of derision burst from the crowd, breaking the tableau. Shouts went up from the commoners as they collectively realized they had been denied any more entertainment for the day. The slaver snatched up the coins and scampered off the platform, dodging and weaving through the crowd of hands that tried to pluck the coins from his grasp and the purse from his belt.

Royce took a knee beside the girl and put a rough hand under her chin. A shock went through his fingers, traveled up his arm, and down his spine, settling into the pit of his stomach like a writhing sickness. Whoever this girl was, she had power to spare.

They would have time to discover the nature of her power later. For now, they had to get off the platform and away from the commoners. Things were growing ugly, and quickly.

"Get up," Royce grunted, unlocking her shackles from the block. "I own you now, so you're my responsibility."

With some effort the girl got to her feet. The glance she shot Royce was wary and vengeful. He owned her now, this demon, full of rage and fire. Royce shook his head. What in the name of nine different hells had he been thinking? He had purchased the girl outright, so she belonged to him. Now all he needed to figure out was what he was going to do with her.

A rotten tomato slapped into Royce's heavy leather chest guard, spraying him with fermented juice and bits of pulp. Denied their prize, the crowd was rapidly taking on the mob mentality. Assaulting the Constable was an offense that could merit a death sentence itself, but the surging mass of people granted anonymity and they were angry.

Royce drew the long dagger from his belt and grabbed the girl by the arm, ignoring the second jolt that coursed through his thick frame. He all but dragged her from the platform into the torrid sea of flesh. He swept the blade back and forth, forcing the crowd to yield before them as they made a hasty retreat from the square.

"My cottage isn't far," he grunted to the girl as they passed out of the throng and into the relative safety of the mostly empty street. "It will be quiet and safe. Then I can figure out what I'm going to do with you."

He felt the girl tense. It wasn't hard for Royce to figure out why. The slaver had said she was untouched. His purchase of her must have made rape seem inevitable. She was, after all, a slave. She was his property, to do with as he pleased.

"Not that way, girl," he said, guiding her down the side street that led to his modest cottage. "I have other plans for you."

~~~~

Chapter 3

Tiadaria stumbled, but the man's vice-like grip on her upper arm kept her upright and propelled her along the sparsely populated road. His touch caused her skin to tingle in a way she had never experienced and made the witchmetal collar burn around her neck. Every time he touched her, it felt as if her skin was on fire. She wanted to run, to get as far away from this village and its people as she could, to find her way back to the north where things were familiar. She would find a place as Klanjon; the expatriate of one clan sworn to serve another. She had heard that some of the clans actually revered their women and treated them with respect. That's what she would do. She would make her way back to her homeland and claim vengeance on her father and the Folkledre of her former clan.

This man who had paid for her would have to sleep eventually, and when he did, she would disappear. Or better yet, cut his throat and be done with it. He may have purchased her from the repugnant little slaver, but he would never own her. She would fight until her dying breath to free herself from captivity and gain her revenge.

They turned down a long, empty dirt road and the man stopped his head-long flight. He released her arm and at once the almost-painful burning tingle that had danced over her skin, vanished. The collar around her throat seemed to expand, letting air into lungs that ached and were starved for breath. She stopped, her hand going to her throat. The man turned to her, his storm-gray eyes ranging over her face before he motioned to a little cottage at the end of the dirt road.

"That's where we're going. Are you going to walk, or do I need to carry you?"

She sprung at him, wanting to grab him by the throat, but her chains made her slow and clumsy. He easily kicked her legs out from under her, sending her sprawling in the dirt on her back. He was suddenly beside her, his knee pressing into her throat and the tip of his long dagger digging painfully into the soft skin beneath her left breast.

"Give me a reason, little one," he snarled at her. "I own you, from toes to teats and everything in between. I can cut your throat right now and as long as you're wearing that collar, no one is going to question a thing. Do you understand?"

She glared at him in silence. She wouldn't give him the satisfaction of an answer and there was nothing he could do to make her. He glowered at her and she stared back. She was getting to him. She could see it in his eyes. If she could push him off-guard, he might slip up and she'd have her chance.

His free hand went to her collar and his fingers slipped under the band. As soon as his fingers were between the metal and her flesh, a burning so intense that she thought her skin was on fire spread from her neck down her spine. She arched her back against the agony, her vision going gray around the edges from the unexpected onslaught. Her stomach churned as her body tried desperately to vomit from the pain. She couldn't see, couldn't breathe, and couldn't think. She was going to die.

He ripped his hand from her throat and the pain ebbed quickly. She stared at him through involuntary tears. Tiadaria wouldn't realize until much, much later that the contact had hurt him too, perhaps as much as it hurt her. She gasped for breath, trying to calm herself and settle her still writhing stomach.

"I will walk, Master," she said in a voice that was little more than a croak.

The man shook his head, frowning. "No, not Master. You will address me as Captain, or Sir. Do you understand?"

"Yes, Sir."

He stared at her for another long moment and then stood up. He took the chain between her wrists and pulled her to her feet. Without another word, he motioned for her to continue down the narrow street to the cottage beyond. She paused at the gate, which he unlatched and passed through without a glance at her to ensure that she followed. He was used to his orders being followed directly, she decided. Captain, then, probably wasn't a nickname.

He certainly had the look of a soldier. His arms were thick with cords of muscle and his gray-black hair was cropped close to his scalp, the better to fit under a snug metal helm. He wore leather scale armor, a thick breastplate that was all too recently stained with rotten fruit, and a pair of breeches woven from some sort of thick, coarse fabric.

He held his dagger like a fighter too. He walked on the balls of his feet, almost dancing as the blade reached out from his outstretched hand, cocked slightly to one side. The blade gleamed in the morning sun. It was recently oiled and had no blemish, no spot of rust, and no sign of any neglect whatsoever. Tiadaria decided then and there that this was a man who deserved to be watched very, very carefully. She would have to bide her time and watch for the perfect moment to make her escape. If she rushed her plan, or erred in its execution, she would be dead. She was certain of it.

Tia passed through the gate behind him and closed it, clicking the latch with delicate fingers. She waited behind him as he stood on the step and fished a small brass key from inside his chest piece. The key was tied to a simple length of black ribbon, but there was nothing simple about the key. It was made of brass, and where the teeth on a normal key might have been, there was a strange array of gears, nubs, and depressions. The man slipped the key into the lock and instead of turning it, let go. Tiadaria stepped back involuntarily as the key twisted on its own, a series of metallic clicks and clangs issuing in muted symphony from inside the door.

"Gnomish engineering," he said, with no further explanation. "It opens and closes with my key and my key only. Don't get any ideas."

Tia nodded. She had suffered enough disgrace. She had no intention of showing her ignorance by telling the Captain that she had no idea what a Gnome was, much less why they should be interested in crafting beautiful and complicated doors. There was a click and the door swung inward, the man walked through the open portal.

She wasn't sure what she expected to find after she crossed the threshold, but a simple cottage with plain adornments seemed completely at odds with the marvelous door they had just come through. There was a small eating area with a basin, a cooking hearth, and a simple trestle table and chairs just inside the door.

The rest of the main room seemed to be occupied by the remnants of some long-fought battle. The table surfaces were covered with maps and parchment that spilled over onto the floor, sometimes landing in other piles that were ankle deep.

There were pieces of armor strewn about, some were plain armor that Tiadaria had seen on guards and soldiers on her brief trip south from the clan lands. Others had obviously been modified for purposes she couldn't comprehend. Still more discarded treasures lay scattered about the room. Daggers and swords were propped against tables, hung on pegs, or in the case of one particularly wicked looking dagger, driven through the body of a book stained with something that looked unsettlingly like blood.

Beyond the eating area was a curtain that Tia suspected led to the bathing and bedding areas. The man strode to the curtain, pulled it back and motioned for her to precede him.

A cold coil of dread settled itself around her stomach and she knew, with fearful certainty that her time of being untouched by men had passed. Swallowing against the sudden rise of bile in her throat, she raised her chin and marched through the divider with only a moment's hesitation. If he thought he could take her with impunity, he had another thing coming. A man naked was a man vulnerable.

The curtain led to a small hallway with three additional doorways that were also covered with curtains. He gestured at the one nearest to the main room.

"The bathing chamber," he said with grave courtesy as he pointed at that curtain. Further down the hall, he stopped at two curtains hung opposite each other.

"These are my quarters," he said indicating the heavy cloth hanging from the doorway. "You are not to enter my quarters unless I expressly request your presence, and then, only after you've announced yourself at the threshold. Do I make myself plain?"

"Yes, Ma...Yes, Sir."

The old soldier looked at her for a moment and then gestured to the other curtain, far more thin and threadbare than the one that blocked access to his quarters. "That is your sleeping room. You may arrange it as you see fit."

She held out her wrists and he stood there, as if trying to decide if taking the shackles from her was a good idea. At length, he took a large ring of many keys from his breeches. He flipped through what seemed like an impossible number of keys before he settled on one and used it to unlock the shackles around her wrists. He tossed them through the curtain in the main room. They landed somewhere with a clatter. Now Tiadaria knew why the main room looked the way it did.

She rubbed her wrists, trying to restore circulation. She offered one ankle, stretching it as far as the chain between them would allow. The old soldier laughed without humor.

"I don't think so, little one. I want to hear you coming."

With that, he brushed the curtain to his room aside and disappeared from view, leaving Tiadaria standing in the dimly lit hallway. She stood there, rooted in indecision, trying to decide if he hadn't found her attractive enough to bed, or if he just wasn't interested in her that way. He was a man though, and from everything she had heard in her village, all men were governed by the brain between their legs. She smiled in silent malice. Well, just let him try. She may still be in leg irons, but he had freed her hands and she was sure that she could make him regret trying to bed her with just those at her disposal.

She pushed the thin curtain aside and slipped into the room. Looking around, Tiadaria decided that the term "room" was being far too generous. Her new living space could be adequately described as a closet without deviating far from the truth. A thin, high window slit allowed a single shaft of sunlight to enter the room, offering scant illumination or life to the narrow space.

There was room enough for a small cot, a water jug and basin, and a desk. The desk could only be used by someone seated on the cot, so the cot served double-duty as a bed and a chair. There were two small shelves above the cot, and a small bookcase with two nooks next to the desk. There was an oil lamp on the desk, along with an inkwell, a quill, and a sheaf of blank parchment. At the foot of the cot was a cedar chest with brass hardware. It was clearly the most well-maintained object in the entire room, the rest of it seemingly thrown together without as much as a thought.

Tiadaria traced her fingers across the surface of the desk, etching parallel lines in the dust that had settled there. It was clear that this room hadn't been occupied in quite some time. Still, the soldier had said that she could arrange it to her liking, so she set about trying to determine how to fit all the contents of the room, into the space in such a way that it all made sense. It soothed her troubled mind to put things in order. Once the chaos had been tamed, she found that she had settled somewhat. She still did not trust this man or his intentions, but her cubicle was undoubtedly better than sleeping in the wagon or in a cell with one eye open.

Once the furniture was organized to her liking, she sought for and found a rag under the water basin, which she used to brush the dust from all the surfaces. She took the thin sheet and blanket from the bed and carried them outside through the miracle door, which the Captain had left standing open.

Outside, she had an insane moment of wanting to cast the bedclothes aside and run for her freedom as fast and far as her legs would carry her. Looking around, she noticed that the windows of the man's room looked out over the small yard. Perhaps the open door was a test. She dare not try to escape when he could be watching her at this very moment.

Besides, even if she did manage to escape, where would she go and what would she do? She was a collared slave. No business would employ her and no inn, halfway house, or work camp would give her lodging unless she presented the signed and sealed leave of her Master. The collar made a far more effective prison than the fancy door and the tiny gate. It was a prison that followed her wherever she went.

Tiadaria channeled her rage into a violent snapping of the sheets and blankets. The dust drifted off as if it sensed the anger coursing through her. Seeking the solace of more order, she shuffled back to her room. There she made up the tiny cot as neatly as she could.

Looking around, she nodded to herself. Her room was perfectly livable, even homely. If she was going to lull the Captain into a false sense of security, she would need to play the part well. She could start by bringing some order to the collected chaos of the tiny house. She left her room and listened in the hallway for a moment. She heard no sound. No snores, no footsteps, no indication that she was anything other than completely alone in the small cottage.

As much as she wanted to be angry, this was the first time she could remember that she wasn't fighting with the other children over scraps of food, or being tormented by her brothers. She may be a slave, but being left alone to her own devices had an appeal that could grow on her very quickly.

The chain between her shackles grated loudly on the floor as she waddled down the hall and into the eating area. She was appalled at what she found. The utensils were clouded and dull, having not been given a good scrubbing in quite some time. The pots and deep skillet were crusted over and showed spots of rust here and there. It was obvious that for all the care and upkeep the man lavished on his weapons, none of it carried over into the tools used for making the daily meals.

Tia worked diligently, setting the eating area to order. First she scrubbed the utensils until the cloudiness was replaced by a shine that would rival the most fearsome weapons that were proudly displayed around the room. The heavy iron skillet took much more work, and her arms were aching by the time she had removed the worst of the grime and rust and had set it by the banked hearth fire to blacken. The pots she scrubbed with sand and rinsed with fresh water from the basin, hanging them from a chain rack on the wall.

When she went outside to dump the water, she was surprised to find the sun low in the western sky. Her machinations had taken the better part of the day and she still hadn't seen any sign of the man who had purchased her.

That thought brought back the sudden fury. It flared within her, flashpowder thrown on a bonfire. She was property to be used however her new Master wished, but was that any worse than what she had been?

Tia bitterly thought of her former home, the long lodge in the snowy wastes where she had grown from a child to a young woman. Clan women were used for cooking, cleaning, and bearing more sons. Clan daughters were raised to understand that they were for cooking, cleaning, and bearing more sons. Nothing more. There was no promise in that sort of life. Slave or not, Tiadaria wanted better. More than that, she wanted revenge. She wanted her father, and Cerrin, to suffer for what they had done.

A rueful laugh passed her lips. At least now she wouldn't be expected to submit to any man who decided to pass her way. The clansmen shared women the way they shared a keg of ale. Tia may be forced to submit to the Captain, at least as long as he kept her shackled, but she wouldn't be expected to be on her back for any man that willed it. She doubted that the Captain was known for his ability to share well with others. That thought was somewhat comforting.

Tia wouldn't succumb so easily, but in the absence of her freedom, there was at least protection here. Protection, at least, was worth making herself useful. She would cook his meals and clean his tiny cottage and do whatever was demanded of her to the best of her ability.

She would earn his trust and when he finally believed that she had been broken and was actually his to do with as he pleased, that's when she would strike. He would never see it coming. It was a perfect plan, and she could wait. She had all the time in the world to wait for him to get nice and comfortable with her. The more she gave him, the more she'd be able to take away.

~~~~~

Chapter 4

Royce had hoped that a good night's rest would improve the girl's mood, or at the very least, make her less openly combative. He was disabused of that notion the next morning when she was just as obstinate and aggressive as ever. She skulked around the cottage like a wounded animal, rattling her shackles and intentionally making enough noise to raise the dead. Normally a patient man by nature, Royce had to fight off the notion to grab and squeeze her by the throat until she passed out. At least then, he'd have a couple moments of peace and quiet.

"Enough!" He finally snapped. He had reached and gone beyond his breaking point. If his outburst gave her some small measure of pleasure, then at least maybe it would keep her from acting out for all of ten minutes. He took his keys from a pocket and found the one that would fit the shackles.

"Come here."

The girl eyed him warily for a moment before she shuffled over to him. She offered him a leg and waited patiently as he knelt to unlock her restraints. As he knelt, she seized what she believed to be a rare opportunity. Patience be damned. Her knee came up in a flash and a slower man would probably have ended up with a broken nose. Shifting quickly to the side, he evaded the brunt of the blow meant to disable and instead took it in the side of the head. It rocked his skull and knocked his teeth together, but he had been hardened by far worse blows.

He sprang to his feet, pivoting away from her. Spinning on a heel, he brought his other leg around and slammed his boot into the top of her foot. She gave a satisfying scream and stumbled backwards. Another spinning kick caught her in the stomach, knocking the wind out of her in a rush. She crashed into the wall and slid to the floor, her eyes dull and glassy.

"I may be three decades your elder, little one, but I'm stronger, faster, and more agile than you. If you aim to kill me, you better practice your stealth and subterfuge. You are clumsy and you have no style. You're not even a worthy opponent. You fall easily and without effort. Hardly a challenge."

The light returned to her eyes and she glared up at him, flashing a hand gesture in his direction that was better suited for brothels and taverns. If nothing else, he thought with a shake of his head, he had to respect her tenacity. She wasn't going to stop fighting him without being broken first, and until she learned when not to fight, she wouldn't learn anything else.

"Do you want these?" he asked, holding the keys just out of her reach and jingling them. Mocking her with them.

She nodded.

"Then come get them." He placed the keys on the table and stood, his arms crossed across his wide chest.

The girl pushed herself up, slowly sliding back up the wall to a standing position. She was still shackled, which was going to make any attack she made that much more difficult, but he wanted to see her try. There was a lot he could learn just by observing and it wasn't in her nature to back down. She would fail before she turned away from the fight. Royce was certain.

Her eyes flicked to the wall beside her and Royce tried to guess which weapon she'd grab first. Nearest to her hand was a long halberd, lying horizontally on the wall across its pegs. She hefted it experimentally and winced, but didn't cry out. Royce knew that pain well; he had felt it every day of his life.

There was a naturally occurring phenomenon that plagued all quintessentialists, those who channeled the raw forces of magic. Mages could not wield weapons of iron or steel. Even close proximity to the metal was enough to disrupt their tenuous connection to the Quintessential Sphere; the realm of time and essence, from which all magic flowed. That disruption, like a fire in the blood, was quickly fatal to the quintessentialist. In minutes, or hours, eating away at their mind until there was nothing left but an empty shell.

Royce was different, as had been his father, and his father before him. Iron affected him not at all, and the ravaging effects of steel were held in abeyance by some peculiarity of his blood.

He was a swordmage, one who could wield a steel blade in one hand and the full power of the sphere in the other. It was a fearsomely powerful concordance of skills, but one that came at a terrible price. The disruption that came to all mages came also to the swordmage, it just came slower. A glacial crawl opposed to a flash freeze.

Tiadaria possessed the same peculiarity of the blood. He had known it from the first time he touched her. The link-shock that coursed through their bodies when they touched was the power of the sphere dancing between them. Now she stood before him, learning to master the pain. He

saw her knuckles go white and watched the
tip of the wicked blade as it sliced a wide arc
toward his mid-section.

At the apogee of its stroke, he took a
single step back, neatly avoiding the
slashing weapon. Her lips curled back
against her teeth and he grinned at her,
mocking her.

"Come child," he teased. "Don't you
come from the Frozen Frontier? I thought all
the clansmen were fearsome fighters?
Oh...but you're just a girl, and a baby at that.
I guess I shouldn't expect you to put up
much of a fight."

Her eyes narrowed and Royce knew
that his goading was getting to her. She was
stubborn, and resourceful, but she lacked
patience. Something that he could exploit
and would get her killed if she wasn't
careful.

Another swipe of the blade and another
step back. This time, she didn't hesitate as
she brought the blade back across their path.
She was driving him back. She wanted him
out of reach of the keys so she could snatch
them up. Let her think she was succeeding,
he thought. She'd have that much more to
lose when she realized her error.

One final swipe of the blade brought her
within arm's reach of the keys and she
dropped the halberd, lunging for the ring. As

the weapon fell, Royce caught the shaft with the tip of his foot and flipped it up into his hand. Careful that his grip didn't slide down into the blade, he spun in a tight circle, slamming the pole into the small of her back and knocking her forward over the table. The keys spun out of her reach, sliding off the table and landing near the hearth.

Easily reversing the weapon, he advanced on her with malice in his eyes and a sneer of contempt twisting his lips. She rolled to one side, trying to avoid the tip of the blade as it came very near her unprotected face. She rolled until she was up against the wall and had nowhere to go. Stone on one side and steel on the other, she was trapped in the truest sense of the word.

"Yield," he demanded, pressing the tip of the blade against her throat.

"No," she snarled and slid sideways, kicking up her legs and fouling the blade of the halberd in the chain of her shackles. Twisting the lower half of her body, she wrenched the weapon from his grasp. Momentarily free from threat, she snake-crawled toward the keys.

He let her get her hand within a few inches of the key ring before he seized her by the hair, putting a knee in the small of her back and the blade of his belt dagger to her exposed throat. He drew his blade across, ever so lightly, drawing a bead of blood that slipped under the blade of his knife and down the pale skin of her neck.

"Yield, little one, or die." She was stubborn and full of vengeance, but she wasn't stupid. Royce expected her to yield when she was bested and she did just that.

"I yield to you, Sir."

The tension went out of her body and she went limp on the floor under him. He plucked up the keys and tucked them back in his pocket, then offered the girl his handkerchief, which she used to mop the blood from the superficial wound. He cleaned the blade on the leg of his pants and then slipped it back into its sheath.

"You have a certain amount of raw talent, girl. That move with the chains was brilliant. You need to learn to focus your anger, and you need to learn patience."

She scowled at him but didn't answer. He sat down beside her, his back against the wall. They were almost shoulder to shoulder, but the few inches between them might as well have been the deepest crevasse on all of Solendrea.

"Can you teach me to fight like you do?" She finally asked, looking across the room, pointedly not meeting his cool regard.

"Not if you don't trust me," he replied. It was an honest answer, if a complicated one. He could certainly teach her the techniques without her trust, but for her to live up to his expectations, to his plans, she would need to trust him implicitly.

"I don't," she said quietly. "I can't."

"I know."

They sat in quiet contemplation for quite some time before Royce reached into his pocket and took out his keys. He offered them to her, hanging on one finger.

"How about we work on that? Starting right now?"

The look she gave him was plainly doubtful. Her eyes narrowed and Royce wondered if this vengeful creature would ever trust anyone about anything. "What's the trick?"

Royce sighed. "There is no trick, little one. I'm offering you the opportunity to trust that when I say I'm going to do something, I do it."

"What's in it for you?"

"Not having to put up with quite as much of your nonsense, hopefully?"

The girl sat in contemplative silence for so long that Royce was certain that she was going to elect to keep the shackles instead of trusting him. He really couldn't blame her. She had no idea who he was or what he had done. To her, he was just another man looking to use her for his own nefarious purposes. He wanted to use her, Royce thought. That much was true. The nefarious part, that remained to be seen.

She reached out and took the keys from him. Her eyes never left his face. She watched him like a hawk until she managed to convince herself that he wasn't going to strike out at her, and then she began searching for the key to the shackles. She found it in short order and freed herself of the restraints.

"Now," Royce said, ignoring the girl's reaction as she started at his firm tone. "You will assist me in getting this room put in order. It's gotten out of control."

To her credit, she paused only for a moment. "Yes, Sir."

As he stood, Royce was overcome with a coughing fit so severe that it brought him to his knees. The girl hovered, indecisive, until he waved her off. His chest felt as if someone had filled it with hot coals. With an expansive gesture, he indicated the whole room.

"I need a moment," he rasped as he labored to get to his feet. "You get started, and I'll join you shortly."

He quit the room without waiting for a reply. Tiadaria looked around. Piles of parchment were literally underfoot anywhere she turned. The surfaces of three large trestle tables were covered in maps and fragments of diagrams and drawings. Scrubbing her hands together, she decided that she would start with the maps. Those, at least, she could organize in a meaningful way.

She found some tacks in one of the cupboards and set about arranging the maps on the far wall of the long room, which was unadorned by weapons or armor. The maps that had clearly defined borders, she matched up together and pinned side-by-side. The others she clustered in ways that looked appealing. Stepping back, she surveyed the map wall and sighed to herself. It looked good, she thought, and brought a sense of order to what had been a chaotic jumble.

Next Tia set about the stacks of parchment. Many of the leaves were written in a scratching scrawl she couldn't decipher. Others she could read, but they made little sense to her. Words like flanking, thrust, and parry; she had heard on the edges of the village fire when the men had talked about their conquests, but they had no real meaning for her.

She dared not try to organize the things she didn't understand, so instead she set about making neat piles of each stack laid out upon the floor. Using a single trestle table to organize her work, she weighed down each stack with a smooth stone that she'd gathered from the garden. At first, a path emerged in the disorder, then a finely woven rug. There was a floor here, under all this clutter, she thought with no small amount of wonder. At length, the parchment beasts were tamed and put in their places and she stood, surveying the room.

All that remained were the weapons and armor. There were pegs on the walls, and it was easy to see that some of the weapons should be hung. Others seemed to have no place, and Tiadaria wondered if they were objects of study or if they had been taken in conquest, the souvenirs of some hard fought battle where the old soldier had bested his foe in a trial of combat.

A long bladed dagger rested on the table in front of her and she picked it up, deciding to begin the organization with the items nearest to hand. As soon as her hand closed on the hilt, a painful shock traveled up her arm, to her shoulder, and into her spine. She cried out and dropped the dagger. It fell point down, and sliced through slipper and flesh. The pain was incredible. A thin wail of agony burst from her lips.

"Stay still." The old soldier's voice came from the partition between the main room and the hallway. He was peering at her, but seemed unconcerned that she was bleeding, quite freely, onto the lavish carpet that covered the bare wooden floor.

Tiadaria ground her teeth against the pain but did as she was told. Tears rolled unbidden down her cheeks, but she didn't sob. She kept as calm and still as possible though the pain in her foot was immense and nauseating. Stubborn she might be, but she was still young enough to cry when hurt and frustrated.

Royce crossed the room in quick strides and knelt by her foot, still impaled by the razor sharp blade. He looked at it from first one angle, and then another, and Tia found herself wanting to scream at him to take it out and stop tormenting her. She clenched her jaw, determined not to cry out and show any sign of weakness.

"You missed all the major tendons and blood carriers, little one," the soldier grunted. His voice was harsh, but his touch was gentle. "I'm sure it hurts, but if it's treated well and kept clean, it should cause no more lasting damage than a small scar as a token of your misadventure."

"Please, Sir," Tia managed to gasp, the pain was becoming unbearable and she wasn't sure how much longer she could stand there with the blade sticking out of her foot like a spring bloom.

He went to the cupboard and got a clean white rag, which he tore into long strips. He knelt by her again and laid the strips on the floor between his knees. He looked up at her once more.

"Brace yourself."

The pain of the dagger thrust into her foot was nothing compared to what washed over her as he withdrew the dagger. She clamped her hand over her mouth, willing herself not to throw up. Fresh blood welled about the wound as he pulled the steel from her savaged flesh and soaked quickly through the thin slipper. He removed that, and taking one of the strips of rag, made a small pad which he held firmly over the wound. The other strips he used to hold the pad in place and bound them to her foot and ankle, providing the pressure that his hand had offered moments before.

Tiadaria swooned and the old soldier caught her under the arms with a speed that surprised her. She barely felt the shock that went from her armpits to her spine, as the throbbing in her foot seemed to drown out any other sensation. The old soldier, however, looked distressed, and gritted his teeth in a feral grin as he lowered her into a chair near the dimly glowing hearth. A moment or two in the chair and Tia felt much less gray.

Royce tossed a log into the hearth, prodding the fire back to life with a long iron poker. He disappeared for a moment and returned with a thick, heavy fur that he threw over her shoulders, tucking the ends under her arms. He slumped in the chair opposite her. He looked very tired, Tia thought. Far more tired than a simple afternoon at home should have made him.

He turned to look at the far wall, newly festooned with the maps that she had tacked there. He looked back at her.

"You can read?" he asked, not bothering to hide the surprise in his tone.

"A little," Tia answered, her cheeks going red with embarrassment. "The women in the north are responsible for keeping the records. Writing about doing things isn't an honorable use of time for a man. He should spend his time doing the things that are written about."

"A man would do well to study the written records of those before him," the old soldier remarked, studying her carefully. "How's the foot?"

"It hurts."

"Aye and it will," he nodded. "More tomorrow than right now, I assure you. Every step you take will remind you that you best keep a strong grip on any blade in your hand."

"It hurt me, Sir. I was surprised."

"Yes, that blade is plenty sharp."

"No, Sir," she said, and stammered when she saw his startled glance. "Begging your pardon, Sir. It hurt me before. That's why I dropped it."

"Hurt you how?"

"Like a burning, Sir. When I picked up the blade, it felt as if my arm had caught fire, all the way up to my shoulder. That's why I dropped it. The long blade...the one from...earlier. It hurt too, but it wasn't as bad."

"The halberd has a wooden shaft. The dagger did not. It was your proximity to the metal that made the dagger worse." His gnarled fingers tugged at his lower lip as he stared at her. "Didn't you ever notice how your body reacts to steel?"

"Clan women aren't permitted steel weapons or tools," Tiadaria replied, her voice dripping with contempt. "Steel is too valuable for a woman's hand."

Royce snorted, but maintained his cool regard. They sat that way long enough for Tiadaria to find herself unsettled by the intensity of his gaze. She felt as if she was being judged on more than just her clumsiness.

"What's your name, little one?"

"Tiadaria," she replied with haughty pride. "And I'm not a little girl, Sir. I'll pass my seventeenth name-day three months hence."

"Then you're a little one compared to me, aren't you?"

"I suppose, Sir."

"My name is Royce. I had another name at some point. A family name, an honorable name. It's been gone from me for many years. Now I'm simply known as Royce. Not that you'll ever call me anything other than Captain, or Sir...but you had the right to know who owns you now."

"A name doesn't tell me who you are, Sir."

"Fair enough," he said, pausing to tug again at his lower lip. Then he smiled, the first full-smile she had seen from him, revealing perfect teeth that seemed out-of-place for such a rugged man. "I am Royce, former Knight of the Flame, and Sergeant-at-Arms to the One True King. I led the Grand Army of the Human Imperium for nearly thirty years."

"Which means, Sir?"

"Which means that I've earned the respect of people far more important than you. Watch your tongue, little one. You enjoy a certain amount of freedom here, but if you think I won't beat you for insolence, you're mistaken."

"Yes Sir," Tiadaria replied sullenly. Wrapped in a warm fur by the fire, it was easy to imagine she was back at camp, listening to yarns spun by the old men. A place where she wasn't an equal, but neither was she a slave. Tiadaria and the old soldier watched the fire burn, its shifting weight sending sparks dancing up the chimney.

~~~~

Chapter 5

They spent many an evening that way. During the day, he would require her to attend things around the cottage while he went about his duties as Constable. She was expected to cook and clean and see to the domestic chores. In return, they would share the evenings and he would teach her about battles fought long ago. He helped her learn how to read with more proficiency than she had arrived with. He instructed her in the basics of strategy and tactics.

Playing chess against each other in the evenings became a common pastime. The Captain said it was a royal game and excellent for teaching basic military strategy. Tiadaria found that she was often confused by the words he used, but that she was usually able to figure out his meaning through inference, or through some chance turn of phrase he had used before.

It was during one of these evenings together that Tiadaria discovered, much to her surprise, that her drive and desire to escape had waned, if even just a bit. It wasn't uncommon for her to pause in their duties to ask why he had purchased her and what her purpose was. It was a question that he always dismissed without answer.

They had just finished their evening meal and were lounging in the chairs by the hearth when he made his confession. It was as unexpected as it was sobering.

"I'm dying," he began, his voice soft and rough. "I don't expect you to mourn. Nor do I tell you this to garner any sort of sympathy or compassion. It is a simple and inevitable truth. I tell you this because in order for you to know why you are here, it is an important detail."

"You once asked me who I am. I was the highest decorated soldier in the Imperium for nearly thirty-years. My influence and power were second only to the King himself. I fought in every major engagement, every battle, and every skirmish. Any time a sword was drawn, I was there. Any time a banner was planted, I was there. I survived every conflict, major, minor, and everything in between. I've seen things that no one should ever need to see, but such are the perils of war."

"That's not a complaint. It's an honor. I was proud to serve, as my father was before me, as his father was before him. The difference is I ran out of time. My father proudly served, and retired, and had a wife and children. As did his father before him. I thought I had more time."

The Captain chuckled ruefully. He took the poker from the hearth and prodded at the fire for a while before he continued.

"I never took a wife, never had any children. I'm the last of the line. The last that knows the secrets of my family and the unique skills we bring to the battlefield. The secrets that have kept every male child of my family alive and employed for as far back as anyone can remember."

"I still don't understand," Tiadaria said candidly. Then remembered her place and added "Sir".

"I am the last swordmage, little one. A fighter who carries steel and can wield magic, just like the quintessentialists, the mages and priests."

Tiadaria laughed and then caught herself. The corner of Royce's mouth twitched with a small smile.

"Impossible, you think?"

"Steel and iron inhibit the nature of the Quintessential Sphere," Tiadaria replied. "So it has been, so it always shall be."

"Letter perfect," Royce remarked. "Just as it has been taught in the Academy of Arcane Arts and Sciences for hundreds of years. I guess the clans aren't as far removed from their origins as they'd like to believe."

Tiadaria kept her mouth shut, not trusting herself to reply. Royce nodded.

"You're stubborn. I like that. You remind me of me. I made my father prove it too." He laughed. A real genuine laugh. "He was so angry. I kept making him show me over and over and over. Very well, a demonstration then."

Royce took a dagger down off the wall. It was the same one that she had once dropped on her foot.

Taking an apple from a basket, he tossed it to
Tiadaria

"I'm going to turn my back," he said. "I want
you to toss the apple into the air when you're ready.
Don't give me any warning. Just do it when it
pleases you."

He turned away from her. Tiadaria stared at
him, wondering. Was he mocking her, or did he
actually believe the nonsense he was speaking? She
weighed the apple in her hand and found her
curiosity getting the better of her. She tossed the
apple underhand.

Royce whirled, his hand a blur of motion in the
air. He reached out with his free hand, snatching the
apple before it hit the floor. He was fast, incredibly
fast, but his speed had come at a price. The apple he
held still appeared whole, which meant that he had
missed his target. Hardly the impressive show that
he had obviously wanted to put on for her.

"You missed, Sir."

"Not hardly, little one," Royce said with a
snort. "I don't miss."

He handed her the apple and Tiadaria saw for
the first time that the core was missing and that the
fruit was sliced into eight neatly-interlocking
sections. She turned it over in her hand, inspecting
it from every angle, refusing to believe what her
eyes had seen and her hands now felt. She looked
up at the Captain. He tossed her the core.

"Show me again? Please, Sir?"

The Captain handed her another apple and they repeated the demonstration. It was obviously no trick. He simply moved with a speed that couldn't be accounted for in any way but with magic.

"You're a rogue mage," she finally said, torn between astonishment and horror.

"To some extent," Royce agreed. "I never trained at the Academy. I was never given the Quintessential Trials. All I know I learned from my father, who learned from his father before him."

"That's impossible," Tiadaria said flatly, shaking her head. "Steel inhibits the flow of magic. Quintessentialists can't even wear steel rings and be able to cast. What makes you so special?"

He laughed at her suspicious tone.

"Steel doesn't inhibit the flow of magic," he said in correction. "Not exactly. The pain you feel when you pick up a blade. This blade, if I remember correctly, is a manifestation of what the quintessentialists feel when they are exposed to steel and iron. So it's not really inhibition, its more-
-"

"Aversion," she said, cutting him off. "The steel doesn't stop the magic; the pain stops them from concentrating."

"Exactly right," he said, beaming at her.

"So since you feel less pain, you can still concentrate, and therefore cast."

"Right again."

Tiadaria picked up another apple from the basket. "Do it again, Sir?"

* * *

The sun had just begun to tint the horizon beyond the training field. Tiadaria stood across from the Captain, her arms outstretched, her palms facing the sky as he had taught her. Her eyes were closed, but she could feel the warmth of the sun climbing slowly on its path across the morning sky. She reached out with her mind, counting each of the blades of grass under her feet, seeing every individual leaf that moved in the gentle sway of the trees at the edge of the clearing.

Further out she cast, feeling the roughness of the stones in the small path that led down to the cottage. Feeling the coolness of the water as it rushed in the stream beside the narrow trail. Something flashed at the periphery of her awareness and her eyes snapped open.

Tiadaria saw the glint of the arrow in the morning sun, it spun lazily through the air and she ducked below it with ease. Another arrow crawled toward her on the left; she danced out of the way. Yet another arrow on the right was closer to its mark. The head sliced a thin furrow on her upper arm, drawing blood and knocking her squarely out of her commune with the Quintessential Sphere. Her magic collapsed and the world sped back up to its normal speed, arrows raining down around her as the Captain fired them as quickly as he could fit them to the string.

The assault stopped when the Captain saw she was injured. He slung the bow over his shoulder and walked toward her, plucking arrows from the ground as he approached. She touched her arm and winced at the fire there. The wound was shallow, but the lips had pulled back from the slice and burned at her touch. It bled quite freely for a wound so superficial. Her arm was covered in a thin sheen of scarlet by the time the Captain had reached her.

"Overconfidence will kill you," he said without preamble. "You're lucky you ended up with just a cut and not an arrow in your meat. Did you forget where you were? Who you were fighting?"

As he berated her performance, he was taking a thin pad of cloth from a pouch on his belt. He mopped up the worst of the blood and then held the pad firmly against the wound. His eyes searched hers. His questions were never rhetorical, and she resented the fact that he treated her like a child.

"No Sir, I didn't forget."

The Captain peeled back the pad, peering at the edges of the wound. From another pouch, he took a hefty pinch of fine white powder which he sprinkled over the cut and ground it in. It burned as surely as if he had laid a brand against her bare skin and Tiadaria yelped, grabbing her arm at the surprising pain. Her eyes flashed in mute accusation.

Brushing his palms together to clear the rest of the powder from them, he tucked the soiled pad back into his belt and gestured to her arm.

"The clay is sterile and will keep the wound clean. It will scar. This is desired. Your scars will remind you that you are mortal and fallible, that losing your concentration may also mean losing your head. Do you understand?"

"Yes, Sir." Not that I'll likely use my arm for the rest of the day anyway, she thought, but opted not to say aloud. She had learned from almost her first day with the Captain that his sense of humor waned completely when he was training or performing his other duties.

His role as Constable, she had discovered, was largely an honorary one. The people of the village would often come to him with petty disputes and quarrels, but rare was the time when he was actually required to hand out any real justice or punishment. The few times that she had seen him do so; he had done it impartially and quickly, without any apparent remorse or emotional involvement.

It was a side of him completely at odds with the passionate storyteller who often inhabited the cottage in the evenings. The Captain would re-live spectacular battles and military actions and would retell them with such vivid detail that Tia could often feel herself standing by his side in combat, fighting against whatever enemy of the Imperium he had stood against.

A sudden pain in her rump broke her reverie and brought her forcefully back to the here-and-now. The Captain had slapped her sharply with the broad side of his scimitar and it hurt. A lot.

"Pay attention, little one," the Captain snarled. "Next time it might be the edge of the blade."

Without any further warning, he brought his blade up in an offensive stance. As the blade flashed toward her, Tiadaria looked beyond the physical realm into the Quintessential Sphere. Time slowed and she saw the tip of the blade crawling through the air. She ducked below it, bringing her shoulders parallel to the ground before she drew her blade. It was an old weapon, short, stubby, and much nicked and dinged with the abuse of who knew how many training sessions.

Tiadaria kicked off with one foot, spinning on the axis of her spine, just below his blade. She felt buoyed by the air, buffeted by the gentle breeze of his weapon sliding through the air above her. She brought the short sword up, intersecting his blade. She felt the shock of the contact in every nerve in her hand, arm, and shoulder. He quickly reversed his stroke and Tia had to drop to the ground, and roll away.

In the timeless void of the Quintessential Sphere, seen only through their eyes, they appeared to move at a glacial pace, a graceful dance of gentle curves and arcs that moved like flowing honey. In the physical world, they sparred at such a frenetic pace that, to the casual onlooker, their strikes and counter-strikes seemed to blur together like the beating wings of a hummingbird.

How long they fought that way, Tia couldn't be sure. She felt and ignored the cries for succor of her arms and shoulders as their blades rang together time and time again. He dropped, his legs flashing out in a circular motion that brought his heavy boot into her ankle. She crumpled to the ground, every muscle in her body throbbing with abuse and exertion.

Tiadaria was quite set to wallow in her misery, until she saw that the Captain lay in the grass next to her, his chest heaving. She felt a grudging sliver of pride, in that she had driven the breath from him. He had beaten her, true, but she hadn't made it easy. Her own breath began to slow as her body relaxed.

She sat up and it was then that she realized that the Captain's breathing was far more labored than hers had been. His eyes locked on hers and she saw the pain and fear there. Whatever was wrong, their battle hadn't caused his current state of distress. The blood ran cold in her veins and she scuttled over to him on hands and knees.

"Flask," he panted, his face ashen white. "Belt."

Tia's shaking fingers went to his belt and searched the pouches there, finding the small stoppered metal flask. She pulled the cork free with her teeth, her hands trembling so badly that she feared she might spill whatever liquid the vessel contained.

She put a hand behind his head and tipped it forward, holding the flask to his lips. He struggled to drink, managing to get the first sip down in an audible gulp that Tiadaria felt through the back of his head. He swallowed again, and then shook his head. She took the flask from him and, with slightly calmer hands, replaced the stopper. He closed his eyes.

The Captain lay there for a moment, his breathing finally slowing and some color returning to his cheeks. It seemed like a long time to Tiadaria before he opened his eyes again. Those eyes, normally full of fire, were dull and listless.

"Captain?" Tiadaria was embarrassed that her voice broke the way it did, but she had never seen a man reduced so quickly.

"I'll be fine, little one," he replied. His voice was low and tired. To Tia, it sounded as if he was reassuring himself as much as her. "I think we're done training for today."

She nodded, settling back on her heels. He struggled to sit up, resting his blade across his thighs as he gave her a measuring look.

"This is only going to get worse, little one. Are you up to it?"

She wasn't sure if he meant his illness, or the care that came afterward. She decided that it really didn't matter what he meant. She didn't have anywhere else to go. Her training was the only thing that had ever made her feel as if she was good at something, as if she had a purpose. If caring for him after his episodes was a part of that training, then so be it.

"Of course, Sir," she smiled. A tentative thing that danced on quivering lips. "Just tell me what you need of me?"

"Allow me to lean on you until we get back to the cottage...and let's do so quickly. It wouldn't do at all for the people of the village to see me in this state. Can you imagine the damage it would do my reputation?"

Tiadaria had to laugh. That sounded more like the Captain she knew. He seemed to rally the nearer they got to the cottage. By the end of the evening, Tiadaria had forgotten about the incident. That was just as well, it would be repeated more often than she would have liked during their time together.

~~~~

Chapter 6

It was barely dawn when a rapping on the door of the guardhouse roused Lieutenant Torus from a fitful sleep. His back and shoulders were sore and he groaned as he straightened up, the chair creaking underneath him. He had fallen asleep at the table again, poring over troop movements and casualty reports from Aldstock. The elves were riled up about something again. Xenophobic by nature, they kept a fanatical surveillance of their borders, but they'd never been outwardly hostile before. He'd lost two good men to arrow wounds in the last week and a half. Something was definitely changing. The rapping returned, increasing in both speed and intensity.

"Alright! Alright!" He muttered several colorful oaths under his breath as he hefted his massive frame, pushing off on the table to steady legs gone numb from sleeping in armor. His feet felt as if they had become extensions of his heavy plate boots. It was as if his joints had rusted during his impromptu nap.

Torus yanked open the guardhouse door and peered down at the little man who stood on the threshold. He might as well have been a city rat, Torus thought. The black eyes set a little too close together, a nose a little too long and pointed to be attractive, even for a man. He wore simple dyed linen, much patched and still fraying in many locations.

"Yes?" the lieutenant demanded peremptorily.

The little man's hands worried at the wide brim of the floppy hat he clutched between dirt-stained fingers. He looked back over his shoulder, and then back at the lieutenant, clearing his throat incessantly.

"Um, sir, the villagers, they, uh..."

Torus ground his teeth. Getting angry wasn't going to help matters. He knew that as soon as he raised his voice to this quivering creature in front of him, that it would be completely useless trying to get any worthwhile information out of him. He stood aside and swept his arm in a wide gesture.

"Please, come inside."

He was unaccustomed to any type of civility, Torus realized as the man stepped sideways past him into the guardhouse common room. The lieutenant pulled out a chair and gestured, a bit firmly, for the man to take a seat. He poured a cup of spiced wine from the skin warming by the hearth and passed the tin cup to his guest. The man's thin fingers grasped it as if he had been handed a holy golden chalice. He took a sip of the wine and sighed. Some of the rigidity left his frame as the hospitality and the drink began to have the desired effect.

"How can I help you?" Torus asked, deciding to try a soft touch.

"Well, sir, the villagers asked me to come to you. They...we...know that you have men down by the tree line. We, uh, we think something may have happened to them."

"Why do you think that?"

The man swallowed, his throat bobbing up and down in a nervous tick that threatened to drive Torus past the edge of his patience.

"Sir, we was doing a bit of trading with your boys. You know, sweets and ale and the like, and we goes down there to play at dice sometimes. We ain't looking to get them into trouble..."

"Whatever trouble they get in, isn't your concern, now tell me why you think something's happened."

"Yes, Sir. We was going to take some bacon down to your boys this morning, but there's no fires and the tents is all pulled down and grass is all torn up around the camp. We didn't get close, on account of them wood-dwellers still being around. They shoot arrows at us if we is gettin too close to the trees."

Torus swore under his breath and the man reddened. The violence with which the man's hands started shaking threatened to splash the wine over the rim of the cup. The lieutenant reached across and plucked it from his grasp, setting it firmly on the table.

"You'll take me there, immediately."

Martin F. Hengst

Torus grabbed his helm from the shelf above the table and picked up his long sword from the rack beside the door. It was a well weathered weapon, with many dings and scratches. It had been his since he had been sworn into the guard as a youngster and had served him through his entire service. The feel of it sliding into the scabbard slung over his shoulder was comforting and brought a sense of peace to him that few things did.

He reached up and pulled the rope that led to the bell in the barracks. The loud pealing echoed through the room and the mousy man clasped his hands over his ears.

"Get up, you lazy bastards!" Torus roared down the hallway. "There's trouble and we need to see what kind."

To their credit, his soldiers appeared through the doorway momentarily, pulling on plates of thick leather armor and buckling on scabbards and quivers. They presented themselves to the officer with a crisp salute, which he returned before he looked them over. Not bad for an emergency muster, he thought. He pulled a strap here, untwisted a buckle there, but the three kids in his charge were as ready as they were going to be.

It was fortunate that the path down to the tree line wasn't too far from the guardhouse. The nearer they got to the forward camp, the more nervous the villager became. Before long, they reached the split rail fence that separated the village proper from the wide swathe of land that marked the border between the Imperium and Aldstock, the ancestral home of the elves. The villager refused to go any further, showing a surprising amount of backbone that Torus wouldn't have believed he possessed had he not seen it.

Torus wondered for a moment if the man or the villagers hadn't had something to do with the attack, but that didn't add up. Why would the man have come to tell them that something was amiss? Certainly they'd have tried to avoid the confrontation altogether. Besides, the man was genuinely afraid of going any further toward the camp. They had been there before, playing dice, so there was no reason that he should not want to return unless he really felt there was something wrong.

From the gentle slope above the camp, it was obvious that there was something amiss. The tents, normally pulled taut against their supporting poles, sagged limply toward the dew-covered ground. The fire rings had been scattered and no whisper of smoke scented the morning breeze. Clothing and cookery items were scattered about. Most disturbing, however, were the weapons that lay, abandoned, around the camp.

Whatever had happened here had happened quickly and with the element of surprise. Torus drew his sword, prompting the others to ready their weapons. Two archers and two swordsmen suddenly seemed like long odds. It didn't help, Torus thought, that these boys were as green as spring grass. None of them had been in combat and spilled blood. Shooting an arrow at a training target was one thing. Shooting one at something that shot back was something else entirely.

He motioned silently to the archers, who nodded and spread out on the ridge. Another gesture and the boy with the sword fell into step beside him. Their approach to the camp was agonizingly slow, eye and ear alert for the slightest warning or indication of danger. As they neared the closest tent, Torus knew they would find no survivors here. The wind brought the smell of sewer sludge, tinged with the thick coppery smell of spilled blood. It was the smell of death. Torus had smelled it on enough battlefields to know that whatever had happened here had been a massacre. He didn't look forward to what they would find.

Torus nodded to the boy, urging him into position across from him, outside the flap of the nearest tent. The lieutenant flipped the flap open with the tip of his sword. The boy beside him dropped his blade and promptly vomited into the grass by his feet. As a soldier, Torus judged him harshly, but as a human being, he couldn't fault the boy. Inside the tent, a scattered mass of flesh, tissue, and bone that had once been one of their brothers-in-arms. Whatever had torn him apart had done so some hours ago. The offal was already beginning to blacken with decay. The stench was nearly overwhelming.

A shout went up from the ridge, and Torus whirled, his blade at the ready. A man stood at the edge of the tree line. He was naked from the waist up, his muscular arms held high above his head. In one he grasped an ornate bow. In the other, a bunch of arrows. He wore breeches of forest green and brown boots that seemed to blend into the ground where he stood.

He walked forward in measured steps, never dropping his eyes from Torus' face. Torus sheathed his sword. He knew an armistice when he saw one. Besides, the look on the elf's face was raw enough that Torus could recognize it even at this distance. He was terrified.

"You may call me Dendrel," the elf said as they came within speaking distance. "My people are not responsible for this, certainly you see that?"

"Torus," the lieutenant replied, gesturing over his shoulder. "I'm not certain of anything, but I've never heard of that kind of brutality from your kind."

The elf shook his head, sadness reflected in his oval, deep blue eyes.

"Our people aren't so different," he said slowly. "This, I think, is a common enemy, if an old one."

"Then you saw who did this?" Torus was growing impatient. If the elf or his kin had seen who the attackers were, they could pursue them immediately and call up reinforcements from elsewhere along the line. Even to Dragonfell and Blackbeach if need be.

"Yes. Your men were slaughtered by the Xarundi."

It took a moment for that thought to register. For a moment, Torus was certain the elf was mocking him and his hand went to the hilt of his sword. The elf dropped his bow and arrows in the grass at Torus' feet, looking up at him with those sad eyes.

"You're mad." Torus's voice had dropped to a hoarse whisper.

"If only I were."

The elf moved to the side, slowly lifting the flap to the tent that was sagging there. Deep score marks marred the tent post. A footprint in the soft dirt was reminiscent of a dire-wolf, but far larger.

"A wild animal," Torus said, half-heartedly. The answering look the elf gave him was no longer sad, but disdainful.

"What animal do you know of that walks on two legs, like man, and has such deadly claws?"

Torus didn't answer. He had nothing to say.

* * *

A mass of black shapes moved along the road toward the village. The pack was silent and only stood out from the night's blackness when the moonlight fell on sleek fur or reflected in luminescent blue eyes. They loped along easily, covering the distance between Aldstock and the sleeping town as fast as a man on horseback.

The leader stood eight feet high, a full foot or so taller than the tallest of his closest kin. He loped along on powerful hind legs, thickly roped with muscle and designed for springing with terrible speed on unsuspecting prey. His arms were equally powerful, with huge hands and fingers tipped by razor sharp claws that slipped in and out of their sheaths with unconscious agitation.

Glowing blue eyes were set above a narrow muzzle and strong jaw. The Xarundi's ears were erect and swiveled two and fro, alert for any sound that might indicate danger or detection. He smelled the stench of man and his nose twitched in hunger and anticipation.

"Where?" growled one of the pack in the guttural tongue of the Xarundi. The language was harsh and sounded very similar to the dialect of their simpler lupine cousins. A series of growls, yips, and snarls served to convey the basics of language.

"Close. Can't you smell the reek of them?" Zarfensis wrinkled his nose in distaste. The settlements of man were growing entirely too close to the ancient forest. They would need to be shown their proper place and made to respect their rightful masters. Snarling quietly, the High Priest called the clerics up from the rear ranks. Their magic would be needed. First to confuse and cause panic among the prey, second to heal any of the Chosen who might be injured in the struggle against the pink-skinned, hairless, vermin. The infestation spreading across the land like wildfire.

They were near enough to the settlement now to make out the sentries as they patrolled on the high wooden wall that surrounded the little village. Zarfensis called the darters forward and snarled an order. Four Xarundi raised long, hollow tubes and, as one, fitted darts into the near end. Each feathered dart was tipped in a poison so potent that a mere drop would cause a sleep that lasted for days and might never end. The amount of poison on each dart was enough to kill a fully grown Xarundi. A human would have little protection against its effects.

"Fire," Zarfensis growled.

There were muted thumps as each darter fired his weapon. Up on the wall, the human guards slumped over at their posts. One fell over the outer wall, hitting the ground below like a sack of vegetables collapsing in on itself.

"Now," the High Priest growled, dropping his jaw in a grin. "We eat well tonight."

The Xarundi closed the distance to the heavy wooden gates with a speed and ferocity that would have terrorized the people of the village, had they had any warning. Without the guards at the top of the wall, the only alert the village would have would be the splintering wood of the Xarundi pulling the gate apart. A feat which they performed with little resistance, as their sharp claws tore easily through wood and pitch.

The gate fell, and the Xarundi poured into the village, pulling down lanterns and torches as they went, plunging the village into darkness. They crashed into doors, knocking them off their hinges and filling the night with the screams of the panicking villagers. As others began to awaken and run, the powerful wolf-men ran down their quarry, tearing out their throats and gorging themselves on the blood and flesh of their prey.

A few of the humans tried to put up a fight, but the clerics made short work of them with spell and staff. The entire attack was over in less than an hour. Every living thing in the village lay dead or dying, except the Xarundi. Slowly, the pack began to reform around the High Priest.

"Orders, Your Holiness?"

Zarfensis's long black tongue flicked out, cleaning off the blood and gore that dripped from his long talons. Once they were clean, he turned to his second in command.

"Collect the offal and set it to burn. Then burn the village. I want nothing left standing."

~~~~

Chapter 7

"I just can't," she screamed, throwing the blade down in the grass by her feet. She wanted to cry and in truth, she was dangerously close to tears, but she didn't want to give him the satisfaction.

The Captain just stared at her, his lips set in a thin, white, disapproving line. She knew she was disappointing him, but they had been training for four hours and she was sore and tired and frustrated.

"Pick up your weapon."

She took a little too long to follow his order and she paid for it with a sharp slap of the broad side of his scimitar across the backs of her thighs. She yelped, and this time she did start to cry.

"I don't understand why this is so important to you anyway," she sobbed. "Maybe you are wrong!"

"I'm not wrong," he said quietly. "You need to focus. You need to center and stop getting distracted. Only then will you be able to channel your power."

Tiadaria bit her tongue. She wanted to tell him exactly where he could stuff his center and his power and even his scimitar. She had told him off once. Exactly once. She'd had the bruises for days afterwards. There were times when she thought that "training" was just a synonym for "thrashing". At least, that's what it felt like.

"On your guard, little one," the Captain said, shifting effortlessly into an offensive stance.

She raised her sword, resigned to taking the beating he would no doubt dish out in response to her stubborn outburst. Then she noticed the men at the edge of the training field. Her grip went slack, the sword nearly falling from her fingers.

The Captain turned to look over his shoulder, seeing that she wasn't being obstinate this time. He sheathed his scimitar and crossed the training field in long strides.

She watched the men talk from a distance. He was shouting, she could hear his voice from where she stood, but she couldn't make out the words. His posture was menacing, his arms flailing about in emphasis of whatever he was saying. Her stomach lurched in response to his mannerisms.

He was agitated and getting more so by the second. One of men dropped a hand to his belt dagger and the Captain took a step back. His hand went to the hilt of his scimitar, but the taller of the men, clad in a voluminous gray robe, raised a warning hand. He said something to the Captain, who looked at Tiadaria. He shook his head, his face set in an angry scowl.

Whatever was going on, it wasn't good. Tiadaria knew the beginning of a fight when she saw one. She had seen more than one brawl in the longhouses and it wouldn't be long before the conflict at the edge of the field came to blows. She wasn't going to wait around to find out how it turned out. She plucked her practice sword from the grass, turned on her heel, and set off in a dead run.

There was a shout behind her and she knew, without looking back, that whoever these men were, they planned to run her down. The edge of the training field was thickly wooded with dense conifer growth. If she could make it into those protecting boughs, she could circle around and meet the Captain back at his cottage and find out what exactly was going on.

Her lungs ached with the effort of keeping her legs pumping toward the wood. The felt the pressure of the air change on her left and she ducked right. She was thirty feet from the edge of the wood. Just a little longer and she would be safe. She could slip into the wood and—

Her frantic thought was cut off as something slammed into her shoulder, spinning her around. An invisible blow slammed into her stomach, knocking the wind out of her and sending her falling backward over her own feet. She crashed into the ground, her head snapping forward as she hit the drought-hardened ground. Tiadaria's world went black.

She floated back and forth between states of consciousness. Things would lighten for a moment and then slip away. She could smell dirt and blood, but everything sounded as if she was underwater.

Somewhere in the distance, she heard the Captain calling her name. He sounded upset.

Tiadaria wanted to tell him that she was okay, that she was just very tired, but she couldn't seem to open her eyes, much less make her mouth work. She heard someone tell the Captain that she was alright, that she would recover completely in a few hours. Of course she would recover. She had just fallen down.

Suddenly she was seven years old again. Even though she had been scolded time and again about climbing the watchtowers, she had picked her way to the very top of the tower that overlooked the valley. She had stayed there most of the day, only climbing down as the sun was slipping low to the horizon. Her brothers thought it would be fun to teach her a lesson, so they waited at the bottom of the tower and shouted at her, scaring her, as she descended. Her foot slipped off the cross-rung and she fell fifteen feet to the frozen earth below. Her brothers hadn't known what to do when she wouldn't wake up, so they ran to the village and brought their mother and father. It was scant consolation that the boys got just as much of a punishment as she did. She'd had a headache for days.

Tiadaria felt a pressure on her head and then warm breath in her ear. It was the Captain and he was whispering something to her, over and over.

"I'll come for you. I promise."

She tried to tell him that she understood, but she was too tired to fight against the coming darkness. She gave in and was still.

* * *

Tia woke with a splitting headache that made her stomach churn. She felt as if any movement, no matter how slight, would set off her sickness, so she stayed as still as possible and kept her eyes closed. She had no idea how long she laid there, but eventually the nausea subsided and she was able to sit up without retching.

She sat on a thin, threadbare mattress on a plain iron frame. The walls were lichen-covered stone and damp to the touch. The air was cool and carried an unpleasant odor of mold, urine, and stagnant water. A black web of mildew traced its way across the side of the mattress. The only light came from a flickering torch on the wall outside her cell.

"Hello?" she called tentatively. The only response she got was her own voice, a faint echo down what must be a long corridor.

What had happened to her? She remembered seeing the men at the edge of the field. She remembered the Captain telling her that he would come for her, but the rest was awash in a murkiness of memory that she just couldn't shake.

Over time, her headache began to subside. As it did, she found that there was a distinct pain in her throat where the witchmetal collar touched her skin.

She worked a finger between the collar and her throat, trying to ease the discomfort, but that only seemed to make it worse. It was tolerable, for now, but she hoped that she wouldn't be here for long. Whether it was the iron bars, or a remnant of the blow to her head, she just wanted it to stop.

As frustrated and angry as she had been at the Captain during their training, she wanted nothing more now than to be with him. In the field with a sword in her hand, or anywhere that isn't here. She thought longingly of their comfortable nights around the hearth, exchanging tales and adventures. Her sword, obviously, was nowhere to be found. There was no way out and she had no weapon. Once again, she was imprisoned against her will. When will I ever be free?

Tiadaria began to cry.

"Now, now, girl. No reason for all of that." The droning voice came from the man she first recognized by his robe. The Magistrate was leaning on a long wooden staff and peering into her cell. She hadn't heard him approach, being rather involved with her own problems.

"Easy for you to say," she snapped, drawing the back of her hand across her eyes. "You're not the one in a cage."

"True," the main replied, nodding sagely. "You'll be free soon enough. We just have the matter of some paperwork and you'll be free to go."

Tiadaria was suspicious. She had never heard about any paperwork from the Captain, and he was as much an expert on the laws of the land as anyone she had ever heard of.

"What paperwork?"

"Just the rightful registration of ownership. Captain Royce didn't enter into a proper contract when he purchased you. There was no sealed agreement."

"What does that mean?"

A stocky little man stepped out of the shadows, large gems on each finger reflected the flickering light of the torch in its holder. Cerrin smiled, the slaver's feral grin full of malice and hatred.

"It means that you are being returned to your rightful owner, slave."

The little man hooked his thumb at his chest, still grinning. Tiadaria shrank away from the cell door until her back was to the wall. She slid down to the floor, too numb to speak.

* * *

Royce ground his teeth as he raced down the path between the training field and the cottage. There had never been much love lost between himself and the Magistrate, but now there was open animosity. There may not have been a letter-sealed bargain for his purchase of Tiadaria, but it had been a legal transaction.

The Magistrate was just looking for a way to stick it to him. He would learn, soon, that he underestimated the lengths that the Captain would go to protect the girl. Legal bargain or not, Royce wasn't going to let Tiadaria go back to that slaver. Cerrin was exactly the type man would want his revenge and he would take it out on Tiadaria in unthinkable ways. There was no way Royce was going to allow that to happen.

He fished the key from around his neck and tried to fit it in the lock, but it wouldn't budge. He tried again, to no avail. Dropping to one knee, he peered into the lock. Someone had shoved clay into the mechanism. Unleashing an endless stream of profanity that had been cultivated from the seediest bars and taverns in the land, he rooted around beside the house until he found a suitably thin twig to dig the clay out of the lock. He didn't have time for this. Every moment he wasted here was a moment that the slaver would be farther away.

Royce ground his teeth together in impotent fury. Of course. That was part of the plan. It had to be. He wondered if the sneaky little rat had known he would come back to the cottage, or if it had just been a lucky guess. Regardless, it was costing Royce time that he really couldn't afford to lose and he'd see to it that the slaver paid this debt thrice over.

He fitted the key into the lock and this time it did its trick, though protesting profusely. Normally a series of ticks and pops accompanied the unlocking of the door. This time, there were squeals of stressed metal and grinding. Royce didn't like the sound of that and he wasn't sure he'd ever get the door open again, but he didn't have time to worry about that now.

With nimble fingers, he donned the thick leather armor that was his daily wear. He exchanged his training blade for the fine scimitar that he preferred in combat. He crossed to the cabinet and flung it open, slinging a black leather quiver over his shoulder. He all but ran down the hallway, through the curtain into his room. From the rafters he took an intricately carved longbow. Sliding the tip of the bow against his instep, he bent the top of the shaft and hooked the waxed sinew over the other end. The string made a satisfying twang as he strummed it. He slipped the bow over his shoulders and went to the stable.

Out on the trade road, Royce pulled up on the reins and brought the stallion around in a slow circle. He stood at a crossroads. There were two main routes out of King's Reach. North and south. If Royce were a betting man, he'd bet south. The slaver had already been north. Had already visited the Frozen Frontier and taken everything there was to take. South would take him through the heart of the Imperium and eventually to Dragonfell. Slaves were an unwelcome commodity in Dragonfell, but there were plenty of little towns and villages between here and there. Cerrin could probably unload his cargo in any number of them. Then he'd have heavily lined pockets when he arrived in the capital.

Spurring his mount onto the southern track, Royce dug in his heels. They rode for such a long time that Royce began to doubt his instinct. He was ready to turn around and try to catch up on the northern track before he saw a thin curl of smoke climbing into the darkening sky of evening. There were no other signs of travelers along the road. He urged his beast into the woods and tied the reins to a low tree branch. He paused only long enough to take a feed sack and a handful of oats from his saddlebag to settle the horse.

It was full dark before Royce found the slaver's wagon. He lay on his stomach on the ridge, surveying the scene below. A number of girls, chained wrist to wrist, were seated on a fallen tree, huddled together. He suspected this was more for comfort than for warmth, as the night was mild and a large fire burned in the center of the makeshift camp.

Tiadaria was there, and Royce sighed with relief. Her arms were pulled up over her head, new shackles looped over a branch that kept all but her toes from touching the ground. Her face was drawn and haggard. Dried blood caked her lips and her left eye was hidden in a swollen mass of black and purple bruises. Her torment pained him, but the fact that the slaver was taking sadistic pleasure in drawing out her torture had given him time to come to her rescue.

"Hang in there, little one," he whispered to himself. "Just a little while longer."

In the clearing, Tiadaria turned her head ever so slightly, as if she had heard him. Then her chin fell to her chest and she went slack against her shackles, her arms pulled up at a grotesque angle.

The door at the back of the wagon banged open and two men appeared. The slaver Royce immediately recognized. The other was unknown to him. They were passing a bottle of amber liquid back and forth, laughing loudly at words Royce was too far away to hear. Every time they roared, the girls seated on the tree would shudder and shift closer to the wagon. The tall, unknown man crossed the clearing at a trot and punched Tiadaria in the stomach, sending her swinging against the shackles. Her head snapped back and she screamed; it was a high, unearthly keening that Royce had heard before. He had watched enough men die to know that sound and know it very well.

Royce had had enough. He picked his way down from the ridge, careful that no loose scree or dead twigs give away his approach. The tall man had become bored with his singular torment of Tiadaria and had returned to the fire and the bottle that waited for him there. Royce circled the clearing, coming up on the dark side of the wagon, using its shadow to hide him from the view of the girls and the men. The fire would work to his benefit, dazzling their eyes and making the shadows that much darker.

He waited for what seemed like hours. The tension was driving him mad. He wanted to act, and act quickly, but he hadn't stayed alive through so many battles by being rash. True, he probably could have taken the two drunkards without much effort, but the risk was too great. He dared not gamble Tiadaria's safety against his vengeance.

Just as Royce had decided that he couldn't wait any longer, the tall stranger got to unsteady feet and announced that he needed to relieve himself.

"Piss on them!" Cerrin called from the fire. "The lot of 'em aren't worth the price of piss anyhow."

The slaver and the tall man shared a good laugh. Seeming to take this advice to heart, the man stepped up toward the terrified girls and hooked his thumbs in the waist of his breeches.

Royce's dagger slipped out of its sheath without a sound. The old soldier half ran, half sprang toward the man as he struggled with the drawstring on his pants. Seizing the tall man by the hair, he wrenched his head back and drew the blade across his throat. The girls screamed as they were sprayed with blood spurting from the slit throat.

Turning to the opposite side of the fire, he saw that the slaver had gotten to his feet, knocking the bottle over and spilling the last of its contents into the dirt by his feet. The stain on the ground looked remarkably similar to the stain that was rapidly darkening the crotch of Cerrin's fine pants. Seeing who had appeared on the other side of the fire, recognition dawned on the little man's face and he

made the only smart decision he could. He turned
tail and ran.

Royce slipped the bow from his shoulder and
drew an arrow from the quiver, seating it and
pulling it back in a single fluid motion. He laid the
feather against his cheek and closed his eyes. He
gazed into the sphere, correcting his aim through
the sightless eyes of the ancients. His eyes snapped
open as he loosed the arrow. It flew straight and
true, slamming into the slaver's shoulder and
sinking an inch into the soft flesh.

The little man bleated like a wounded animal,
but still managed to get to his feet. It was an
impressive act for a man in the grasp of strong
spirits. Royce fitted a second arrow and repeated his
shot, sinking an arrow into the opposite shoulder.
The man crumpled, screaming. Without his arms to
rely on, he lay face down in the dirt as Royce slung
the bow back over his shoulder and walked toward
the spot where he fell.

He lifted the man under the arms and dragged
him back to the edge of the fire. He pulled the
arrows free, none too gently, and pushed the slaver
into a sitting position against the cart's wheel.

"Your keys," Royce demanded. "Where are
they?"

The slaver looked up at him, his eyes showing
far too much white.

"In...the...wagon," he panted, struggling for
breath.

Shock was setting in, Royce thought. Thankfully, it was taking its time. He wasn't done with this little man who made himself feel big at the expense of little girls. He yanked the door open and climbed inside. A small candle lamp illuminated a table and benches, no doubt where the girls would sit for their ride to whatever destination full of horrors they had in store for them. A makeshift bed took up the front end of the wagon, its linens stained and none too fresh.

Royce's hatred for the slaver abruptly matured as he reached over the foul bedding and took the keys from the nail driven into the corner post. As he exited the wagon, he kicked the man in the shoulder as he passed, causing a renewed round of screaming.

He glanced at the girls as he passed. They had subsided into weak sobbing. Royce felt for them, but Tiadaria was his primary concern. He ran to her and unlocked the shackles, taking the weight of her body in his strong arms as she fell limp against him. She opened the one eye undamaged by the beating and her split lips parted in a weak smile.

"You came, Sir."

"I promised you I would, little one."

"No one," she said, laboring to form the words. "No one ever keeps promises to me."

"I do."

Royce shushed her then and carried her to the fire. He laid her as near to the flames as he dared and turned to the slaver. He had gone white and

Royce knew that he wasn't long for the world with or without his help. Now that Tiadaria was safe or relatively so, he found that his thirst for revenge had subsided.

He went to the man and hunkered down, taking his dagger from his belt as he did so. "I'm going to give something you never offered these girls," Royce said, gesturing to them with the tip of the blade. "A quick death."

"Please!" the man gasped, struggling to sit up. "I can pay you, anything you want, girls, money, name it and it's yours."

Royce snorted with derision. He plunged the dagger deep into the man's chest, gave it a savage twist to ensure the wound was mortal, and then wiped the blade clean on the little man's tunic. Sheathing the knife, he checked on Tiadaria and then went to the other girls, who shrank back from him in unison. He kicked the body of the tall man out of the way and went to his knees before them.

"I'm sorry," he said. "I'm sorry for all that you've had to endure at his hand and that you had to witness things that no gentle girl should have to see. I can't promise that I can get you back to your families, but I can get you back to King's Reach and you can find your way from there."

Without waiting for them to reply, he went to the slaver and plucked the jewels from his fingers and the purse from his belt. He treated the tall man the same way, finding no lack of coin in his purse either. It would be enough to give these girls a new life.

It took him a long time to free the girls and usher them into the wagon. By the time he got Tiadaria into the bed that he spread with fresh grass to cover the worst of the stains, the smoke of the burning bodies was climbing into the lightening of the morning sky.

~~~~

Chapter 8

Tiadaria lay in her cot, listening to the bird sing right outside her high slit window. She wasn't sure how long they had been back at the cottage. The first few days of her recovery had been a haze of pain and semi-consciousness. Then the infection had set in. She knew that the Captain rarely left her side, and when he did, it was to summon the best clerics and priests to practice healing magic or say prayers on her behalf. He was beside her cot, morning, noon, and night, and she didn't know how he was managing to stay with her and still adjudicate the tasks that his position as Constable required of him.

Her fingers idly picked at the soft woolen blanket that was spread over her. Though summer hadn't yet passed into fall, and the days were still warm, she found herself cold more often than not. She wondered if the cold was in her head. Her thoughts kept going back to the tree that she had hung from and every time her thoughts turned in that direction, it was like being doused in cold water. She didn't want to show any weakness to the Captain, lest he lose his faith in her, but whenever he left her alone in the house, she was beset by panic.

Then there were the dreams. It seemed like every time she closed her eyes, she saw Cerrin and his friend taunting her, mocking her, telling her in graphic detail all the horrible and vile things they were going to do to her before they finally cut her throat and left her to bleed in front of the other girls. An object lesson in what happens when you disobey your master. She felt the gorge rise in the back of her throat and she swallowed hard against it, determined not to be sick yet again.

She was miserable. She wanted to put the whole thing behind her and yet it seemed like everything she did reminded her of that night. Tiadaria wondered how long it would be before those memories faded and worried that they might be with her for a long time. Tears slipped from the corners of her eyes. Try as she might, she couldn't keep them from coming.

The Captain had appeared with a laden tray, but as soon as he saw her wet cheeks, he deposited it on the desk and went to one knee beside the bed. His hands hovered over her and his face was a mask of anxiety that pained Tiadaria almost as much as her injuries.

"What hurts?" He asked quietly, his voice soothing her jagged nerves.

She shook her head.

"Nothing, Sir," she said, equally quiet. "I just..." She trailed off and looked up at the window, not knowing how to explain, or even if she had to.

He laid his hand on hers and she knew that she didn't need to say anything else. The shock that used to be painful was now a reassuring reminder of their bond. It was the thing that told her that though they were different from everyone else, they shared something unique between them.

She wondered if that bond was what had helped her to hear the Captain's voice in her head before he swooped down to her rescue. She hadn't built up the courage to ask about that yet. Everything seemed so hard these days. Even the slightest things were a huge undertaking and she just wanted things to get back to normal.

"Are you hungry?" He gave her a thin, tight-lipped smile. "I've done the cooking, I'm afraid. I may have rescued you just to put you in the ground again."

Tiadaria couldn't help but giggle. It was a weak, thin sound and she hated how vulnerable it made her seem. Still, any laughter at all was a good sign, she decided. At her willing nod, he pulled the tray from the desk and settled it onto her lap, helping her sit up to better take her meal.

The Captain's lack of culinary skill had become something of an in-joke between them. Tiadaria had told him that since he was so used to cutting things apart, that he should naturally make a good cook. Alas, he said, this wasn't so. He was old and tough and stringy and any meal he attempted to turn out was often reflected upon the same way by those unfortunate enough to be served.

There was a thick beef broth on the tray with thinly sliced vegetables. Her stomach rumbled, not with nausea but with actual hunger. It was the first time in days that food even sounded appealing, much less looked or smelled it. She wasn't sure if the Captain had outdone himself, or if she was just so very, very hungry; but the soup was excellent. She drank every bit of it, even bringing the bowl to her lips with shaking hands to finish off the savory liquid.

The Captain stayed with her throughout the meal, nodding with approval as she finished what he had put in front of her. He seemed to appraise her before he took the bowl from her fingers and placed it on the tray, whisking it out of the room, the very pinnacle of efficiency. What he was taking stock of, she couldn't guess.

As he left, the now familiar pang of panic chilled her guts and made her long for his return. This won't do. Not at all. How am I going to survive if I fall to pieces every time he leaves the room? I'm here, I'm safe, and I can do this. She steeled her resolve and forced herself to breathe deeply; concentrating on the movement of her chest and the mild pain the bruises still caused her as she pushed air out of her lungs.

The Captain returned, hooking his foot around the stool in the corner of the room and lowering his big frame onto the tiny wooden tripod. For an instant, Tiadaria thought it was going to give way under him and he was going to crash to the floor below, but aside from a mighty creak as he settled his weight, nothing else happened.

"Sleep, little one," he said softly, stroking her hair back from her forehead. "I'll be right here."

* * *

A heavy pounding on the door to the cottage awoke Tiadaria and set her heart to a similar rhythm. It was still full dark outside the high slit window to her cubicle and she fumbled around on the bedside table for the box of matches there. She lit the oil lantern and holding it out before her like a ward, slowly crept down the hallway toward the common room.

Just as she was about to pass through the curtain partition she felt something slip between her neck and the collar, giving her a nasty shock. She screamed, as much in surprise as in pain, and a heavy hand clamped down over her mouth. How she managed not to drop the lantern in her panic, she'd never know. The old soldier's face was rough-hewn in the harsh light.

He laid a finger to his lips and locked eyes with her, ensuring that she understood his silent command. She nodded quickly and he released her, motioning for her to let him past. He preceded her into the room and walked quietly, on the balls of his feet, to the front door.

When Tiadaria had arrived in the cottage, she hadn't understood why someone living inside the village would have fit their home with such heavy bronze shutters on the inside of the windows. Now, however, she was thankful for the protection they offered and glanced around the room, ensuring that the heavy wood planks that held them shut were in place and that all was in order.

The Captain had explained to her in no uncertain terms that the duty of securing the house every night fell to her, and promised dire punishments if she neglected any part of that task. She was glad that she had taken those warnings to heart and double, even triple checked that things were in order after their evening meal each night.

The pounding came again and Tiadaria jumped. Whoever was outside was worried not one bit about waking up half the village with their shenanigans.

"Constable!" The voice that came from the other side of the door was high and laced with panic. "Constable! Please! Open up, Constable. It's horrible, absolutely horrible."

The Captain went to the door and drew back the brass plate over the view slit. He peered outside for a moment and then threw the bolt, taking the key from around his neck and unlocking the intricate lock from the inside. A moment later, he yanked the door open and the young man standing on the threshold all but fell inside.

Tiadaria had seen uncontrolled panic before. During a raid by a rival clan, she had seen the men set fire to the long houses in which the women and children were taking their meal. Tiadaria had been lucky enough to have been sent into the pasture that morning to gather the cattle. She arrived back at the village just in time to see her mother and young brother fleeing in panic from the burning structure. They had survived with only the most minor of burns. Others weren't so lucky. The anguish and fear that had overtaken her clan was clearly mimicked on the young man's face that stood before the Captain now.

"Constable," he sobbed. "Please, you must come at once. Something horrible has happened in Doshmill. The bodies are all burning and the houses too. There's nothing left standing in the whole village. The priests found a single child, a girl that had been stuffed in a water barrel and hidden under a bed. She said there were terrible monsters that came into the village and..."

The boy faltered, going even whiter. Tia was positive that he was going to faint dead away. He swayed on his feet and the Captain caught him by and elbow, steadying him with one massive hand.

"And what, lad?"

"And they were eating people," the boy gasped in a low whisper, his eyes spilling over with fresh tears. "She said they were eating people alive."

Tia closed her eyes at his anguish and couldn't help but see in her mind the cattle she had found in the pastures periodically. Often the youngest, weakest, or slowest would be savaged by the large wolves or snowy lions that inhabited the rocky crags that surrounded her ancestral home. But what could do that to an entire village? And how quickly would it had to have happened, so that one young girl was the sole survivor of the massacre?

"You've done as you ought, Bryce. Go back to your father and tell him that I'll be along shortly. We'll ride for Doshmill immediately. This can't wait until first light."

"Yes, Constable."

Having a message to relay seemed to steel the boy and set his nerves right. He nodded jerkily to Tiadaria and slipped past the open door and into the night. The Captain pushed the door shut with one foot and leaned against it, scrubbing at his face with both hands.

He stopped and looked at her. She was still standing, just inside the common room, holding the lantern. In honesty, she didn't know what else to do. Her mind still reeled with everything she had heard in the last few minutes. Even then, she didn't know what her responsibilities were. Beyond cooking, cleaning, and occasionally running to the market on errands for the Captain, she hadn't done much of anything. They had their near daily training sessions, but she suspected that these were more to keep him in shape than to teach her anything.

During her recovery, the Captain had regaled her with tales of battles fought long ago. He had a wonderful knack for storytelling, filling in details and gaps that placed her on the battlefield, with all of its sights and sounds and smells. She could feel the cold steel in her palm and smell the stench of death when he spoke to her of all the things he had done in his youth, the things he had done in service to the Imperium and the One True King.

To say that she thought him the bravest man she had ever known wouldn't be inaccurate or an exaggeration. Though she knew her own father to be tough and wiry, skilled in battle, she also knew that if the Captain had done even a fraction of the things he claimed to in his stories, that he was a consummate fighter to be feared by all.

The Captain never boasted. In fact, if his tales were lacking in one detail, it was his direct involvement in the battle, maneuver, or raid. There was no question that he had been there. The depth and breadth of his explanations and ruminations couldn't be questioned. He had commanded many men and had watched more than a few of them die. He had given the orders that sent them to their deaths. Tia knew that those lost souls still bothered him, for when he spoke of the dead he did so in hallowed, hushed tones and then was quiet for a long time afterwards. Sometimes, those lapses into silence indicated the end of the evening. They would stare into the fire until it died into embers. He would dismiss her then, sending her to her cubicle while he finished the night in quiet solitude.

She was torn. Some nights she wanted to go to him and offer whatever small comfort she could. Other nights, she was furious with him for keeping her in this cottage, away from the world and whatever else she might find there. Her anger, she had found, served no purpose. She was owned and wouldn't be free, even if she escaped. The collar would remain with her for the rest of her life. A symbol of her shameful status and a warning to others that she didn't act with her own free will.

"Go get dressed," the Captain said, his harsh voice startling her out of her thoughts and making her jump. "We must prepare for battle."

"Now!" he roared as she hesitated, and Tiadaria scampered down the hallway to her room.

She threw open the chest and quickly shucked her thin nightshirt, replacing it with underthings, a pair of plain doeskin breeches, and a pale green tunic. This she wrapped twice with a belt and knotted it above her left hip. She slipped into her boots, supple leather with woven wool inners that felt soft and inviting against her bare feet.

Tia ran back down the hall to find the Captain staring at the maps tacked to the wall, tugging at his lower lip. Although more parchment had been added to his collection since then, he had kept things in the cottage as she had organized them. It was obscurely pleasing that he found her simple tidying helpful. She crossed the room and went to the heavy leather armor that was hung up on pegs to the right of the maps she had organized weeks before.

"Not that," he said quietly. "Look at that armor, what do you see?"

Tiadaria stared at him, unsure of why, when time was apparently of the essence, he would be taking her to task for not knowing his preferences.

"I see leather and brass, Sir."

"Yes," he agreed, nodding. "Leather and brass, but what do you see?"

She glanced at him and then back at the armor on its pegs. She didn't know what he wanted from her, but she was determined not to fail in whatever test this represented. She looked hard at the armor, trying to decipher the mystery he obviously saw there.

"It's thick," she said, deciding to enumerate all the details she could. "The armor is slabs of thick leather, cut in sheets, and fastened with brass. It's bulky."

She paused, not wanting to anger the Captain, but having one final, if impudent, thing to say. He arched one eyebrow, waiting.

"It looks slow, Sir."

The Captain nodded. "Indeed, little one. That armor is slow. Its heavy, meant to deflect a blade or keep it from piercing. It is the armor of a slow, plodding warrior who says, going into battle, 'I am going in this direction and nothing will stop me.'"

"And what armor do you prefer, Sir?"

"This," the Captain said, with an unexpected grin. He opened the cabinet door and took out a neatly folded parcel of cloth.

He laid the package on the table and unfolded the heavy velvet. Tiadaria gasped, for what was revealed sparkled and gleamed like the finest silver the in the lamplight. A tunic of fine silk, overlaid with a fine mesh of tiny rings, lay in the center of the bundle. The Captain put the tunic aside and set out a pair of breeches of the same manufacture. Finally, he laid a pair of slippers out on the table. Turning to the cabinet, he withdrew two of the finest swords Tia had ever seen.

These were not the scimitars that he carried daily. These were awe-inspiring weapons that radiated a power she could feel in the base of her neck. Scabbards of supple white leather held the hidden blades. The guards, pommels, and hilts of the identical blades sparkled with the slightest movement. A golden dragon twined around the dark leather grip, frozen fire forming the guard that met the sweeping curved steel blade that the Captain withdrew a few inches from its housing for her to see before laying the swords and their belts next to his armor.

The Captain dropped his sleeping pants, and quickly slipped into the armored breeches. As he tightened the drawstring, Tiadaria got her first look at his naked chest. She had seen men naked from the waist up before. The men in her clan would often wear less than this in the drum circles around the great bonfires. What she had never seen before was a man with so many scars.

They stood out against his tan skin in bright relief. They crisscrossed his arms, his torso, and the broad line of his shoulders. There were some that were small and some that nearly wrapped around him. There were those that were straight as an arrow shaft and others that had jagged, torn edges. The ones that mesmerized her, though, were the fine white scars that made up intricate patterns that adorned his body here and there. They were incredibly detailed, obviously intentionally cut and not the result of some random wounding.

He pulled the tunic on next. Then passed the belt around his waist and slipped on the slippers. He stood before her, resplendent in the glory of the finest armor and most intricate weapons she had ever seen. They stood that way for a moment, before he smiled at her, catching her eyes.

"Get our horses, little one. We have an adventure ahead of us."

~~~~

Chapter 9

Whatever Tiadaria expected to see when they arrived at the edge of what had once been Doshmill, a burgeoning village at the frontier of the Human Imperium, she wasn't ready for what they found. Everything in the village had been burned to the ground. The tall wooden palisades, the cottages, the temple, the lattices in gardens and fences around yards. Nothing that could burn was left standing. Those buildings that had been largely constructed of stone were charred and blackened.

The worst thing was the pile of smoldering bones and charred flesh that were the earthly remains of every single human inhabitant of Doshmill except one. The girl who had been hidden away in a water barrel and managed to survive until daybreak. Had she not been tucked away under and old bed in the earthen cellar of the inn, the largest stone structure in the village, it was unlikely she'd have survived either. As it was, she was white and shaking, being attended to by two priestesses when they arrived.

Royce swung from his saddle and handed the animal's reins to the girl, indicating a decent pasture for the horses with a curt nod of his head. His armor jingled quietly as he landed on the balls of his feet and set out with long strides toward the knot of people gathered just beyond where the gates had once been. He pushed his way through the crowd, making his way toward a barrel-chested man with coal-black hair and amber eyes that seemed to drink in every movement and every detail of the people and events around him.

"Torus!"

The man glanced up and as his eyes landed on Royce, broke into a wide smile. He bellowed an order and people shifted out of the way of the giant man, opening a wide path between them. Royce stopped a few steps away and straightened up, throwing off a salute that was instantly returned by the smiling titan.

"It's damn good to see you, Captain," Torus said, thumping the smaller man on the back and threatening to knock him off his feet.

"Constable, now, Torus. I hear you're in the running for the Captain's job?"

"Aye, Sir, but you'll always be the Captain to me. You raised us from pups. Everything I know about battle and fighting and politics," Torus wrinkled his face in an expressive grimace at the last word. "I learned from you."

"You were always a good student, Torus. You didn't call me out here with all haste to talk about old times, though. What happened here?"

Torus Winterborne paused, cocking an eyebrow as the girl came up behind Royce, standing behind and slightly to the left. The old soldier glanced at her out of the corner of his eye and looked back at his former prodigy.

"A slave, Sir?"

The wonder and disbelief in Torus's tone made Royce wince inwardly. This wasn't the time to get into this discussion yet again. He knew all too well the younger man's views on slaves and the slavers who sold them.

"It's a long story, Torus," he said firmly. "It was my crowns, or an executioner's ax."

"Ah," Torus seemed to regain some of his composure. "Well, I suppose that makes things a might different then."

"Circumstances are what you get when you run out of luck," Royce snapped.

The younger man roared, slapping a huge hand on his thigh. It was obviously a remark he had heard before. Royce glared at him for a moment and then started laughing himself. The two stood that way for several long moments, drawing the disapproving glares from several of the people gathered around them. Finally, Torus wiped the tears from his eyes and gestured toward the smoldering ruins.

"It's good that we got our laughter in now, Captain," he said as they walked. "I'm afraid there's not much mirth to be found here today."

"What happened?"

Torus shook his head. "I don't know. Or rather, I hope I don't know. I have a theory that I'm betting you can confirm."

"That doesn't sound good, Torus."

Torus stopped and turned to look at his former mentor. He was worried, Royce realized. Really worried. He was struck forcibly by a memory from years gone by. Torus had been a teenager, and involved in the typical tomfoolery that boys his age were bound to get into. Someone had gotten hurt and that injury, as accidental as it was, had weighed heavily on the young man. Royce thought that he looked as worried and apprehensive now as he had on that day so many years ago.

"It's not, Captain. Not at all." and Torus's voice dropped to a rough whisper. "If all this means what I think it does, it's bad. Really bad. For the entire Imperium."

Royce whistled through his teeth. A village attacked was bad enough. Something bad enough that Torus thought the entire Imperium might be in danger? He quickened his steps and Torus and the girl trotted to keep up.

Crossing over what had once been the threshold into the village, Royce had to press the back of his hand to his mouth. He had experienced every form of carnage known to man, but the stench of a burning body still got him right in the back of the throat. This wasn't just one burning body either, it was what was left of an entire village of corpses thrown into a haphazard pile and set to blaze.

The fire obviously hadn't been tended, as more than a few of the bodies hadn't been consumed by the flames. Royce heard the girl retch behind him and he glanced back to see her doubled over, heaving the dregs of last night's meal onto the charred ground between her feet. He felt for her, but it would do her well to learn this lesson now and harden herself against it. She would face much worse and she would have to be ready. She'd have to develop a stronger stomach for the atrocities of monsters and men.

"This is everyone?" Royce circled the pile of bodies, taking note of which were completely destroyed and which were only partially eaten. If there was a pattern there, he couldn't see it.

"Everyone we know of," Torus replied slowly. "We didn't bring the youngster back into the...well, the ruins. We didn't want to scar her even more."

"Wise."

Silence fell again and Royce continued his careful plodding walk around the perimeter of the bodies. He was pleased when he noticed that the girl had fallen into step behind him, following the same path, walking, literally, in his footsteps. He saw her straighten as her mouth formed a little 'o' of surprise. He turned to her, and she pointed, dropping to one knee.

"This one, Sir. It looks," she swallowed hard. "It looks as if this one has marks."

Royce walked over and knelt down beside her. The stench was much more powerful this close to the center of the pile. He could feel the heat coming off the bodies and he was thankful that the girl had steeled herself for the task that must be performed. He looked where she pointed, to the thigh bone of a young man whose upper half was all but unrecognizable.

"You're right, little one," he said, lightly touching the bite marks on the leg. He grasped the foot, turning the leg gently from side to side. The flesh had been torn from the bone and there were long grooves etched in the red-tinged ivory. "So what eats humans and piles them up to burn the bodies?"

"Wolves?" she asked tentatively.

Torus snorted and Royce shot him a quelling look.

"Wolves don't burn down buildings, little one." Royce looked at her, willing her to make the connection that he had made.

Her eyes went wide and she shook her head, slowly at first, then with increasing fervor. "No. No, Sir. That's impossible."

Royce's smile was humorless.

"Few things are impossible, little one. Most are merely improbable."

"But," she blanched as she looked at him. "But the Xarundi are a myth. They're a ghost story that mothers tell their children to make sure they are home before dusk. This isn't possible."

"Have you ever considered, little one, that maybe every myth has a grain of truth?"

"But," she said again. Her mouth worked silently for a moment before she finally gave up and pressed her lips together in a thin white line.

Royce sympathized with her. It wasn't an easy thing to learn that the nightmares you had as a child were suddenly coming true. If this was a Xarundi attack, and he couldn't see how it could be the result of anything else, it was the first since his childhood. Since his father had been the Captain and he just a little boy tagging along to learn what it meant to be the most powerful fighter in the Imperium.

He remembered the first day that he learned monsters were real and he felt a strong sense of remorse that he was the cause of the end of innocence in the girl. Still, better that she learn now, while he could protect her, then later when he couldn't.

Torus sighed and rubbed the back of his neck with a massive calloused hand.

"I was really hoping you'd have better news for me, Captain."

Brushing his fingers in the dirt to scour off the thin film of blood, Royce stood and brushed his hands together, as if the gesture could not only remove the dirt but also the memory of what they had seen.

"I don't like it either, Torus. There are troubling questions here." He ticked them off on his fingers as he spoke. "First, why this village? What was its importance? Second, why now? Why come out of hiding after thirty years? Finally, what do they want? And more importantly, how do we stop them?"

Torus shook his head, his face a grave mask of anxiety.

"I don't know. I do know that the King needs to know about this right away. I'll ride for Dragonfell immediately."

"We'll go with you."

Torus shook his head slowly.

"I'd welcome your company, Captain. I would. But the girl..."

"The girl," Royce said firmly, "is under my care and protection. Where I go, she goes."

For a moment, Royce was certain that Torus would decide that he didn't need the company after all. He hadn't trained a fool though. He knew that Torus would want his input when they briefed the King. Although slaves weren't well tolerated in the capital city, Royce was confident in his ability to diffuse any unpleasantness that might arise.

"Alright," Torus said finally. "But you might want to warn her first. She's not apt to receive a warm welcome."

Royce motioned for Tiadaria to follow him and stepped downwind, away from the bodies.

"Torus is blunt, but he's right. If we go to Dragonfell, it's not going to be easy on you. Slaves aren't welcome in the King's backyard. There are likely to be those who loudly call for your removal from the city. Some of them might even try to do it themselves. Even so, I would be there to protect you. I offer you the choice, we go or we stay...but either one, we do together."

The girl regarded him for a moment and Royce returned her gaze evenly. He could almost see the thoughts tumbling about in her head and he urged her in his thoughts to stand up to the challenge. He thought she would. She didn't back down from a fight easily.

"We go. I've heard stories about Dragonfell. If the stories about the Xarundi are true, the tales of the grandeur and opulence of the King's palace might be as well. I want to see that! Besides, how many slaves can boast of an audience with the King?"

Royce snorted. "Not many at that, little one. It's not going to be fun and games. It's going to be a long journey and a rough landing at the end. You're up for that?"

She paused only a moment before she replied and Royce respected her calm dignified answer. "As long as you're with me, Sir, I'm up for anything."

"Then we ride for Dragonfell."

* * *

Tiadaria had no idea what had possessed her to agree to such madness. It was well after dark when they finally called a halt to their first day's travel. Her bottom and legs were sore from the hard ride. They had pushed the horses as far as they thought they safely could. All she wanted to do now was curl up in a ball and go to sleep, but the horses needed to be rubbed down and a meal needed to be cooked. These duties, obviously, fell to her.

As she stirred a thin travel stew in a pot that Torus had provided from his saddlebags, she pondered exactly what had come over her to agree to such a foolhardy journey. In a few weeks, the fire of her resistance had died down to embers. Every now and again those embers would flare up and she would remember her indignation at being bought and sold, but for the most part, she served the Captain because it was comfortable and pleased her to do so, not because it was expected of her.

He treated her well and kindly. The only times he was harsh with her were the times, during training, when she wasn't paying attention or was being intentionally obstinate. He had taught her many things about fighting with swords and staves. He claimed that she was helping keep his reflexes sharp and he seemed to genuinely enjoy the practice. However, she had noticed him taking a swig off the flask he kept tucked in his belt all too often.

She had tried to ignore that, but she had found, much to her growing chagrin, that she would miss him if something were to happen to him. He wasn't just the man who had purchased her anymore. He was the man who had saved her from execution, because he thought she could be more. That kernel of knowledge, which she had denied so vehemently at the outset of their relationship, had grown into a strong, sinewy vine of grudging trust.

She finished with the stew and served both men first, then herself. She sat down on a log to eat, and then settled into the grass when she found that the log was far too hard and unyielding to sit on with her sores. They ate in silence, every one of them too tired to do more than gulp down the soup and spread out a bedroll.

As she spread out the thin blanket she kept under her saddle, the Captain approached her from around the fire. Torus was already rolled on his side, his back to the banked warmth of the embers, snoring softly. The Captain hunkered down beside her and motioned to her blanket.

"Lay down, little one. On your stomach."

Tiadaria's stomach dropped suddenly. Was he really going to take her here? In the open, under the stars, with another man a rock's throw away? Tia knew that it was his right, but in the weeks that she had been his, he had never taken a single action that led her to believe that he thought about her in that way.

Her mouth suddenly dry and empty of words to say, Tia silently did what he commanded. She lowered herself to the blanket and pillowed her head on her arms. She was his property, she reminded herself bitterly. She should be happy that he had waited this long. Tears sprang to her eyes, but she was proud that they were as silent as her mouth, slipping out of the corners unnoticed by the Captain.

His deft fingers undid her belt and he laid it slowly aside. His careful, plodding movements almost enraged her. She wanted to scream at him to finish, to do what he needed to do and stop tormenting her, but she couldn't bring herself to make a sound. She couldn't help but tense, however, when his thick fingers slipped into the waistband of her breeches and pulled them down, exposing her bottom to the cool night air.

The Captain reached across her back, snapping a long leaf off a bush there. Tiadaria watched him out of the corner of one watering eye. He took the leaf and squeezed a thick, clear sap from the broken end, coating his fingers with it. Then he gently spread the sap on the worst of her sores. Instantly, Tiadaria sighed with relief. The pain of the broken skin subsided rapidly and before she knew it, the Captain had pulled her breeches back up and covered her with the nape of the blanket.

He knelt down by her head, showing her the bruised end of the leaf that he had used to ease her suffering.

"Remember this plant, little one. You rode long, hard, and well today. You earned those sores you have. Don't think I don't know how much they hurt. I've had them myself from time to time. But the sap of this plant will set you right."

He paused then, a thick finger reaching out to trace the track of a tear, still glistening in the firelight.

"I'm sorry, Sir," she whispered, a new tear rolling out of the corner of her eye. "I thought--"

Tiadaria saw the pained look flicker across his face and in that moment, she hated herself for being the cause of his pain. The tears came in earnest now, her sobs threatening to wake Torus.

"I know what you thought, little one." He laid his hand on her head and the shock of their mutual connection coursed through her.

Over weeks of training, she had come to be able to ignore the sensation for the most part, only noticing it when it was particularly sudden or unexpected. The bond-shock made the hairs on the back of her neck stand up and her spine tingle with anticipation. This wasn't the pain she was used to, but rather a pain-pleasure that made her ache all over.

"You are lovely in every way, little one, but I can't do that. If that ever changes, I promise you that I'll tell you first."

"I am yours, Sir." She looked up at him, her eyes puffy and red from her tears. Their eyes locked and in that moment, Tiadaria realized that she really was his.

The collar was incidental. She was his property, true, but her desire to leave had been replaced by an equally strong desire to serve him and to learn everything that he could teach her. To be with him for as long as he had, and to comfort him when his time was drawing to a close.

"I know," the Captain said softly. "And I will ever be yours, but not that way. I think I told you that once before."

Tiadaria smiled then, remembering their first encounter on the road to the cottage, how he had knocked the feet out from under her and sent her sprawling in the dirt. If only she had known then what she knew now.

"Yes, Sir," she sighed. "I believe you did."

"Get some sleep, little one. Our days are going to be long and difficult for a while and you're going to need it."

With that, he turned from her and went to his own blanket, rolling away from her and sharing the warmth of the fire with Torus. Tiadaria listened to their discordant snoring for a long time before she, too, finally slept.

~~~~

Chapter 10

Royce reined his stallion in and brought it into step with Tiadaria's gelding. The journey had been long and tedious, but she had acquitted herself of it without complaint. Every evening she would care for the horses and make whatever meal was to be prepared for that day.

Then she would serve them before she served herself. In the morning she would scrub the small pot and on more than one occasion, she had gathered fresh berries to help break their fast. If there had been any question in Royce's mind about her suitability as his successor, no doubt remained. She conducted herself with the poise and grace of a highborn lady, though the collar would forever deny her those privileges.

"We're nearly there, little one." Royce smiled at her sigh of relief. She quickly composed her features into an impassive mask, but he understood how she felt. The trip had been longer than he would have liked as well. "Trust me, the descent into Dragonfell will be worth everything you've gone through."

She snorted and he shook his head. The gentle gait of the horse's walk required no thought or effort on his part and he easily slipped into the past.

He could still remember, vividly, the first time his father had brought him to Dragonfell. He wondered if the girl would feel the same sense of awe and wonder as he had. He had been younger and his journey had been much shorter. He hoped that their time on the road wouldn't diminish her enjoyment of the experience.

The rough road pitched upward and they began the steep climb to the top of the last ridge they would encounter before they reached the city. Once they crested the ridge, they would be able to look down into the valley and see the grandeur of Dragonfell laid out before them.

It was said that the Imperium of Man was founded on the backs of the last dragons. The legend went that three brothers, each declaring themselves to be King, would have a contest of sport. Each brother would attempt to find and slay a fierce dragon. Whoever killed the fiercest beast and lived to tell the tale would be the One True King of the Imperium and all of mankind.

The first brother went south to the elven forests, where he found and did battle with a cruel green dragon. The beast was huge and cunning, and the brother was certain that his triumph over the creature would place him in the throne as the One True King. For three days and nights, they battled each other, slipping in and out of the trees and around the wooden city of Aldstock where the elves held their High Court.

The elves turned on the human intruder, for killing any creature of the wood, even a vile and vicious dragon, was forbidden. Beset on two sides, the brother fought with all his skill and cunning to defeat the dragon and the elven King. After a time, he managed to put them both down and brought not only the dragon's head, but the elven King's bow back to the village.

The second brother went west, to the lands of the dwarves in their high mountain holds. He had heard stories of a terrible red dragon that terrorized the mountain folk and demanded sacrifices to prevent his unholy wrath. The brother wandered the mountains for days without seeing the dragon. The dwarves were unwilling to help. They knew it would be their hide that would be flayed if the brother failed and the dragon learned who had betrayed him.

Finally, weary and ready to turn back and admit his failure, the second brother quite literally stumbled into a crevasse and found the giant red beast. His search above had been in vain, for he found the creature guarding a single crimson egg, its shell gleaming brightly in the semi-darkness of the fissure. A fierce battle ensued, for the dragon was fighting not only for its own life, but for the life of its offspring as well.

No amount of battle could save the dragon, and the second brother emerged victorious, striking a killing blow through the heart of the great beast. Rather than take its head, he took the malevolently shining egg back to the village where he met with the first brother. They each boasted of their accomplishments, showing off their treasures as signs of their prowess and worthiness to be king.

Many weeks passed, and the two brothers began to worry, for they had not heard from the third brother, who had set off for lands far to the east. He had traveled so far, it was said, that he had sent back letters with his trusty falcon telling the people of his village of all the wondrous things he had seen on his journey and enjoining them to await his triumphant return.

Still more weeks passed and the two brothers were all but certain of their sibling's demise. They went to the village elders and told them that if their brother did not send word of his safety, or reappear within the fortnight, that they would have no choice but to declare him dead and proceed to determine who would be king without him.

On the third night after this meeting, the third brother's falcon arrived in the town with a map tied to its leg. There was a single line scrawled at the bottom of the map: "Your King waits."

The brothers were furious at such audacity. That their brother had declared himself king without winning the contest angered them deeply. They gathered the elders of the village and every man who could carry a sword and they set out on the long journey to follow the map that their brother had sent. It took them nearly three weeks to complete the trip, at last coming to a high ridge that was marked on their guide. The very ridge that Royce was climbing now.

As the brothers crossed the ridge, they stared down into a green, fertile valley, bounded on the east by the sea and on the other three sides by high ridges and stony cliffs. Laid out in the center of the valley was the largest black dragon any of them had ever seen. The third brother stood tall for a man and still was half the height of the giant head that lay dead in the middle of the field.

As his siblings approached, the third brother spread his arms wide and welcomed them, smiling. "Come," he said. "Tell me of your triumphs and treasures as I share mine with you." Together, the three men walked toward the mouth of a huge cavern set in the northern wall of the protected valley.

The third brother was awed by their stories and congratulated them heartily on their accomplishments. They reached the cavern and the third brother bowed deeply, smiling with pleasure at his brothers' stunned silence. The cavern was a demesne fit for a dragon's unique requirements. It was deeper than they could see and had many tiers both above and below the main level that were stuffed with all manner of treasure, mystical and mundane.

"This, my brothers, is my legacy. We shall bring all of mankind here, and we will make them safe within these walls. We will work the valley and hillsides and we will make an empire for ourselves. This is my vision, as your One True King."

The brothers were unable to argue. Their brother had the strength to rule and had killed the most massive dragon anyone had ever seen in testament to that strength. He had the foresight to rule, as he had already planned out how and where to unite the scattered tribes of men. The two other brothers fell to their knees, bowing deeply and proclaiming their kin to be the One True King.

Royce wondered how much the valley had changed since the time that the three brothers had ruled over the Imperium. The One True King on his throne and the brothers acting as his advisors. Certainly the dragon still kept watch over them all, for its skull was perched on the mountainside, overlooking the facade of the cavern-city. They were nearing the pinnacle of the ridge now and he turned in his saddle to watch Tiadaria expectantly.

As the horses crested the ridge, the girl's face went from boredom to incredulous delight in the blink of an eye. Her grip on the reigns tightened so much that her horse came to a stop in the middle of the path. She gazed down in rapt wonder at the valley below.

It was much different now, even than in the days of his youth, Royce thought. The city sprawl had extended further out from the mountainside. Houses and taverns now mingled with the lush green of the fertile farmland that surrounded the capital city. The facade was still as impressive as ever. Huge alabaster stone works had been raised around the mouth of the cavern, with the dragon's skull perched atop them, nestled against the jutting peak of the mountain. The three brothers, their likenesses carved into towering statues of that same alabaster, gazed out over their city, standing as eternal sentinels over all mankind.

"Oh Sir," she breathed. "It's wonderful!"

Torus snorted, but his smile was kind, if a little sad. Royce wondered what he was thinking. The huge man had grown increasingly quiet over the course of their journey. The last day or so, he had barely said anything at all. Royce fervently hoped that he was just worried about the attack on the village and how that news would be received. It would make sense if that were the case, as his somnolence had grown the nearer they got to their destination.

Glancing at Tiadaria, he was pleased to see that her excitement hadn't faded from the initial burst of wonder she had experienced at the top of the ridge. He wondered if she had ever been to a large city in her entire life. The clans weren't known for traveling outside their territory, and they didn't have any large cities that he was aware of.

He would have to ask, although he was hesitant to bring up her history, for fear of hurting the girl. There were plenty of things that were going to hurt her that he would be unable to avoid, or even be a party to. He wasn't going to do it on a whim.

Whether by habit or intent, Torus had taken up the point position, leading their meager train down the switchback path that led from the pass, to the floor of the valley. The horses seemed undeterred by the steep path and easily picked their way over the few loose rocks that had fallen onto the path from above. This was the portion of the arrival that Royce didn't care for at all.

The path was narrow and there were too many places that a rock could be dropped from above onto an unsuspecting head. That was part of the point of such an approach, he knew. It made good tactical sense, but he preferred to use his tactical sense against others, not to feel like it was being used against him.

The lieutenant gave a low whistle and Royce was instantly alert. He had trained his men to use simple, unobtrusive signals when in dangerous situations and the trill that his former pupil had used urged caution and wariness. He brought his steed into step with Tiadaria's. She looked at him and he was proud to see that she had recognized the signal he had taught her.

"Trouble, Sir?"

"Maybe. I'll find out. In the meanwhile, keep behind Torus and I."

"Yes, Sir."

Royce spurred his mount and brought it alongside the much larger man. He was leaning back in his saddle, trying to ease the uncomfortable feeling that they might pitch forward down the hill at any given moment. He looked sidelong at Royce without turning his head. Royce did the same.

"What is it, Torus?"

"Maybe nothing, Sir." He glanced down over the lip of the switch back and then patted his steed's neck absently. "But maybe something. Two men and horses, down at the head of the trail."

Royce glanced down. He could just make out two forms in the shadow of a large boulder that marked the mouth of the pass leading through the high foothills. Squinting, he found that the horses had been tethered a short distance away and left to graze. Torus had always been long in the eye. He was one of the best archers Royce had ever trained. He dared say that the lieutenant was a better shot with a bow than even he, even taking into account his unique abilities.

"Too far away to tell much," Royce said.

"Aye and it could just be my gut finally catching up to all the worrying I've been doing lately."

They slipped into silence as they continued down the path together. When they reached the bottom of the trail, they found that the two men were merchant-traders, dickering over the price of goods that were coming through the pass by wagon. Royce was relieved that there had been a reasonable explanation for the unexpected overseers of their arrival, but it unnerved him to think that such precaution was even necessary.

He knew that Torus was on edge because of the girl. He expected trouble, and truth be told, they might find it by bringing a slave into the capitol. There were few things that bred distrust and dissension faster and more thoroughly than a slave among the commoners. They felt, and rightly so to Royce's way of thinking, that every slave brought into the Imperium took a job away from a citizen who needed it. This attitude diminished the further one got from Dragonfell, but here, in the heart of the city, it would still be a matter of white hot contention.

Still, he hadn't really had much of a choice in bringing her or not. Realistically, she had nowhere else to go and he couldn't just leave her on her own. She may be growing into a fine warrior under his tutelage, but she wasn't ready for that yet. There were those, even as far outside Dragonfell as King's Reach was, who would seek to make an example of her. He wanted to ensure that she had both ample opportunity and sufficient skill to protect herself from that type of enemy when the time came.

As they approached the first crossroads, Royce finally began to settle. People on the street waved as they passed and if anyone noticed the thin witchmetal collar around his young companion's neck, they didn't call attention to it. It had been many years since he had come to Dragonfell. Maybe attitudes had changed for the better since the last time he was here. Still, it was a city teeming with people and that many people in that large of a crowd had a funny way of letting their neighbors decide what they should think.

The packed earth path became cobblestone, lined with neat little rows of cottages almost identical to his. Beyond them lie the larger buildings of the city proper. There were inns, common houses, and one or two buildings that Royce remembered from the days of his youth as popular brothels. They would pass through the market square and up the high street toward the royal palace, nestled safely inside the walls of the cavern.

Royce dared not take Tiadaria into the palace proper. Attitudes may have changed, but they wouldn't have changed that much. He had the advantage of a purse full of coin, which would buy them a room and entertainment enough to keep her occupied while they finished their business here. They would be ready to move on before long. He hoped.

~~~~

Chapter 11

Royce had to chuckle at Tiadaria's comically rapt expression as they passed through the market square. To someone who had never been outside their village, it must seem like a wondrous, miraculous place. Traders with crates tucked under their arms hawked their wares loudly and constantly, engaging in good natured bickering over the quality and price of those competing against them for customers. There were stalls of all sizes, shapes, and descriptions. The merchants that manned these stalls were as varied and foreign as the wares they peddled.

The spinner's cart was laden heavily with so many bolts of cloth that Royce thought he would be able to fashion a sail for every ship in the Imperium's fleet. There were heavy linens and fine silks and the array of colors was dazzling. Purple, green, and blue in one pile, gold, orange and red in another. Still more combinations were heaped up in the cart, scattered haphazardly as the spinner bargained with the women who were competing for his singular attention.

Next to the spinner, there was a tanner with fine pelts and furs and buttery leathers that looked that they would be soft and warm against the skin.

Then there were bowyers, armorers, and artisans.
The market square was busy and crowded, a sea of
bodies moving with the influence of some unseen
tide. They made way for the travelers, but
grudgingly, as it interfered with their bargaining.

They passed into the farmer's section of the
square and Royce's mouth began to water. They
had lived on field rations for the entire trip and the
smell of spit-roasted meat was enough to set his
stomach grumbling. He edged his horse nearer to
the stall and called over the butcher's boy, buying
three skewers of beef glazed with a sweet-savory
sauce. He tossed the boy a half-crown from his
purse and waved off the need for any change. The
boy scampered back to his Master to share his good
fortune at such a generous purchase.

Royce passed the skewers onto Torus and
Tiadaria and the three of them ate in silence as they
wound through the streets toward the great statues.
When he was finished, he licked the sauce from his
fingers and wished that he had gotten twice as many
of the sticks. Oh well, he mused, there would be
plenty of time for eating after they had spoken with
the King. He would see that Tiadaria got a good
meal at the inn. It was likely, it being as late at is
was in the day, that they would be invited to break
bread in the palace. That wasn't an invitation that
one dismissed out of hand.

It wasn't very long before they left the market
square behind them and Tiadaria looked over her
shoulder, her face a mask of wistful longing. Royce

wished that he could just give her some pocket money and turn her loose to experience what the city offered, but he knew he couldn't. The city would be dangerous for her. Not only because of her status as a slave, but because she wasn't used to so many people in so confined a space. The narrow alleys, twists, and turns could be disorienting for someone who hadn't seen more than a handful of stone buildings in their entire life.

At last they came to the inn that Torus had recommended. He told Royce that he would go on ahead, but meet him in the palace as soon as he had set his affairs in order. Royce nodded and said that he would be along as soon as he had settled the girl.

This late in the afternoon, the common room of the inn was mostly empty. There were a few older men playing at dice in the corner, but the evening patrons who would come for a hot meal and cold ale hadn't yet begun to arrive. A young woman with fire red hair and eyes so green that Royce thought they could have been cut from emeralds stood behind the bar, rubbing oil into the worn wood. The girl was wearing a high-collared frock that made her look much older than her years. She looked up at them as they approached, her welcoming smile turning a trifle colder as she saw the collar around Tia's neck.

"A room, please," Royce said firmly, ignoring the look of disapproval. "Two beds, if you have it. A bed and a cot if you don't. Two nights."

"We book by the week," she replied shortly. "Two crowns. Two and a half if you want meals too."

He pulled his purse from under his belt and withdrew a five crown piece. The coin was thick and heavy, the namesake crown embossed on one side and an underscored numeral five on the other. He placed it on the counter and pushed it toward the girl, who turned it over in her hand for a moment before it disappeared into her apron. She produced a ring with a single simple key and pointed to the stairs at the end of the common room.

"Third floor," she said without a trace of her previous animosity. "All the way at the end of the hall, room twelve. My name is Ecera, if you need anything."

"Thank you, I'm sure we'll be fine."

They stopped by the livery to retrieve their saddlebags and then climbed the common room stairs to their floor. There were only four rooms on the top floor of the inn, and theirs was the furthest away from the rest of the customers and lodgers. This suited Royce just fine. The fewer people that knew who they were or that they were there, the better. Things were going to be bad enough when he and Torus spoke with the King. He didn't need to be compounding problems.

Once inside, Royce slid the bolt into place. The room had two beds, a table, and not much else. A hand printed card on the table listed meal times and directions to the outhouse, which was behind the inn proper, near the stables. He tossed his saddlebags on the table and looked at Tiadaria, who was standing by the window looking out over the city.

"I need to meet Torus at the palace. Stay in the inn until I get back and then maybe we'll have time to see the city."

"Yes, Sir," she replied, without turning from the window. There was an odd hitch to her voice, but Royce shrugged it off. She was probably still in awe of everything they had seen so recently. He paused a moment, torn between wanting to stay with Tiadaria and ensure that she was settled and discharging his duty to Torus and the King. In the end, his honor won out, and he turned on his heel and left the room, pulling the door shut behind him.

* * *

Tiadaria heard the door click shut behind her and she waited until the Captain's footsteps faded away before she released a long, wavering sigh. She hadn't wanted to cry in front of the Captain. She didn't want him feeling bad for things he had no control over. Still, the attitude of the girl behind the counter had hurt her in a way she hadn't been expecting.

Torus had warned them that things might be made difficult by her collar, but she had chosen to believe...believe what? That he had been lying? That somehow she was different? Her questions were answered only by bitter tears, which she swiped away angrily

Slave or not, she had had the opportunity to see the most wonderful things on their way into the city, she reminded herself. There were those, especially among her clan, who would never see the city of men, much less be able to stay there. She had never seen as much coin as she had during the few weeks she had been with the Captain. Her father, the Folkledre of her clan, had once shown her the entirety of the clan's fortune, which amounted to about ten crowns.

The Captain carried five times that amount as a matter of course. Things were much different here. In the clans, one made what one needed, grew it, or did without. During the trade festivals in the spring and fall, the clans would gather to barter for items from the other tribes, but during the rest of the year, a clansman was expected to be self-sufficient.

For the first time, Tiadaria felt as if she was far from home. It wasn't just the distance, either. She felt as if she was becoming more accustomed to being with the Captain than she had ever been with her clan. She had vowed that she would become more than a slave. Hadn't she started down the path to just that end? She had learned to fight and was getting better at it every day. She had traveled to the most important city in the Imperium with a former servant of the King and his current Lieutenant. If she wasn't shaping up to be more than a simple slave, the company she kept certainly said otherwise.

There was a soft rapping at the door and Tia jumped in surprise. She went to the door and slid the cover of the eye slit back. It was Ecera, the girl from the counter. Tia frowned. There had certainly seemed to be no love lost between the fire-headed girl and herself when she arrived, what could she possibly want now? Comforted by the fact that she was probably a much more skilled fighter than the boarding girl, she opened the door a crack.

"Listen, I'm sorry we got off on the wrong foot, may I come in?" There was a pause. "Please?"

Squashing down her fighter's instincts, Tia opened the door and allowed Ecera to come into the room. They were maybe a year or so apart in age, Tia thought. Ecera had seemed so much older when she had been talking to the Captain, but that was probably just her demeanor. She seemed genuinely contrite now and nodded courteously to Tia as she stepped into the room, her coarse brown skirt swirling around her ankles.

She plunked down on the bed and looked at Tia expectantly. Unsure of what to do, Tia pushed the door shut with a click and sat down on the bed opposite the one that Ecera had perched on.

"You don't say much, do you?" Ecera asked, her head cocked to one side. She regarded Tia for such a long time that she began feel her face flush with embarrassment. "It's okay," the boarding girl continued. "My father, he owns the inn, says that I talk enough for three old spinsters anyway. I'm pretty sure I can hold up my end of the conversation and yours."

"Oh," she said, before Tia could get a word in. "Your Master asked me to bring you this." She took a gauzy scarf from her belt pouch. Slipping from the bed, she arranged it around Tia's neck, hiding the collar from those who might casually look her over. "There you go," she said with a small smile. "Much better."

"Thank you," Tia said, her voice very quiet.

Ecera cocked her head to the other side, peering at her. Tiadaria was starting to get frustrated. She hated feeling as if she was some object of curiosity to be studied. She was about to snap.

"You're not like other slaves I've seen," the innkeeper's daughter declared in final judgment. "You're much prettier and much less black-and-blue."

"The Captain treats me very well," Tia said, somewhat defensively.

"I'm sure he does," Ecera replied, patting her knee awkwardly. "He trusts you a lot. I've never known a Master to leave a slave to her own devices without chaining her to the floor."

"The Captain has never kept me in chains," Tiadaria replied, stiffening. "Not since the days just after he..." She trailed off. She had never admitted to anyone else that she had been sold. It felt strange and unpleasant and she found herself wishing that she hadn't opened the door in the first place.

"The days after he bought you," Ecera said. She leaned forward and laid her palm against Tia's cheek. Tia, startled by the unexpected show of compassion, withdrew from the touch.

"It's okay." Ecera's voice had taken on an odd roughness. She reached up and pulled down the collar of her frock, exposing the thin metal band that encircled her throat.

"You're a slave?"

Ecera nodded.

"I am. Well," she chuckled without much warmth. "I was. Father sold me when the inn wasn't doing so well. He used the money to turn things around and he bought me back from my...from the man who purchased me."

Ecera said the last few words in a rush, as if it hurt her to say them, or even think them. Tia's mind was drawn back to the wagon in the woods and the horrible, painful death that the slaver had promised her. She shuddered.

"It wasn't so bad," Ecera said, mistaking Tia's shudder. "Just...some Masters aren't as kind or thoughtful as yours. I wouldn't go as far to say you're lucky...but you're luckier than some."

"I'm sorry," Tiadaria said, and she meant it. For all of her anguish at being taken as a slave and kept against her will, the entire ordeal had brought her to the Captain, who had done nothing but treat her with relative kindness and teach her. She dared to guess that she was a better tactician now than even her father. She was certainly more skilled with a blade.

"It's okay," Ecera said briskly, rubbing her hands against her skirt as if she could brush away the painful memory. "I'm home now, and that's all that matters. I may forever be a slave to everyone else, but at least I have a roof over my head and my family back. Some of us don't even get that much."

"Why not just have your collar removed?"

Ecera looked at her with surprise.

"It never comes off. Didn't anyone tell you that?"

Tia remembered the slaver telling her that she would be marked forever as a slave, but she obviously had never had the inclination to ask exactly what that meant. She had never thought to ask the Captain either, and he had never volunteered the information. A sudden bitterness welled up in her like poison.

"No," she replied sullenly. "No one ever did."

Ecera's eyes searched Tia's face. Her expression was one of pity and that was almost harder to deal with than the realization that she would be collared for the rest of her life. She didn't want Ecera's pity, or anyone's. Collar or not, she was stronger than any woman she had ever known.

Tia's defiant train of thought must have been obvious. Ecera looked at her closely and pursed her lips in a determined line.

"Do you know why they call it witchmetal?"

Tia shook her head. Ecera sighed.

"I really don't want to do this, but if it'll keep you out of trouble, I'll show you, just this once." She slipped a finger between her neck and the collar. "See this space? Just about a fingertip. Yours is the same way, right?"

Tia nodded, not at all sure where this was going and feeling more than just a little apprehensive. Ecera sighed, taking a short knife from her belt. Tia started in alarm, but the girl just smiled sadly.

"It'll be okay. Just do please pay attention; I don't want to do this more than once."

With that, she struck her collar with the cap of the knife. There was a dull metallic thunk and to Tia's amazement, the collar shrunk until it bit into Ecera's throat. She gasped for breath, falling back on the bed, her fingers instinctively clawing at the metal band. After a moment, the collar returned to his previous diameter, and Ecera took several deep breaths.

"So," she said panting. "Now you know. That was just a quick rap with my blade. Hit it with a hammer, or a sword and it might kill you. I saw it happen."

"I really am a slave forever, then," Tia said. Her voice was cold and had a bitter edge that sounded strange, even to herself.

"Yes," Ecera replied sadly. "And no. You'll always have the collar. It doesn't mean you'll always be a slave. It just means that you were once."

"I'm not sure there's much difference."

Ecera shrugged. "I'd rather have a collar and my life than the other way around."

She stood, smoothing her coarse skirt down over her legs as she did so. "Anyway, I need to get back downstairs. If you go exploring, do be back before your Master returns. I don't want him, or father, angry with me."

She bobbed a curtsy and slipped out the door, closing it behind her with a snap. Tia stared at the door long after Ecera had retreated back down the stairs. If you go exploring, she had said. The Captain had told her to stay in the inn, but he had also asked the innkeeper's daughter to bring her the scarf to hide her collar. Surely that was a form of tacit permission. Besides, she wouldn't go far. She just wanted to get out and stretch her legs a little. After the disappointment of the afternoon, learning that she would never be free of her collar, it seemed like a perfectly reasonable thing to do.

~~~~

Chapter 12

The last time Royce had been to the palace, it had been the day he retired from the Grand Army of the Imperium. That memory was bittersweet. He had given the best years of his life in service to King and country, but if he had known then that they would be a prelude to his final years, he might have done things a little differently. Still, what was done was done. No sense in being drawn down about it now.

It was good to walk through the streets of Dragonfell again. Being in the city reminded him of being young and running errands for the knights in the Grand Army. He had grown up at his father's knee, learning strategy and tactics and becoming the fighter that his father had always planned for him to become. How had he never had a son to pass on that legacy to? No matter, he was making up for it with the girl. The girl who shared his unique talents, but not his blood.

Royce had never put much stock in fate or destiny. The thought of some invisible hand guiding him to this choice or that was unsettling at best and downright disturbing the more he thought about it. However, there was no other good explanation for how he had come to stand on that execution platform on the day the girl had been brought before the ax man. Even if he had been a betting man, he wouldn't have taken those long odds. His arrival at the palace proper snapped him out of his reverie.

Torus was leaning against the portcullis wall, cleaning his fingernails with the point of his belt dagger. It was a nervous habit that Royce recognized from the lieutenant's training. To all outward appearances, he seemed to have not a care in the world. Royce knew better. He sighed. Why was nothing ever easy?

"Is it really that bad?" he asked at he closed the distance between them.

"It's that obvious?"

"To others? Probably not." Royce nodded at the blade. "To me? Yeah. It's pretty obvious."

Shoving the blade into its sheath, Torus jerked his head toward the granite stairs just beyond the portcullis. "Guess we should go find out exactly how bad it is," the lieutenant said with some resignation. "But I doubt it's going to be a social visit."

"I suspect you're probably right. So let's get it over with, shall we?"

The two men climbed the stairs in silence. The guards outside the palace door waved them through into the opulence of the main hall. Either they were well enough known, or expected, or both. Royce doubted he had been away from the city so long that all of his legends had died out. The thought brought a smile to his lips and Torus looked at him skeptically.

"You actually like this, you old mercenary. The Imperium might be under attack and you're reliving days of past glories."

"Not exactly."

"But close enough," Torus groused.

"Yes," Royce agreed tolerantly. "Close enough."

The rest of their walk down the great hall was peppered with nods and waves. There were foreign dignitaries, members of court, and artisans milling about. If the King was concerned about the attack, Royce thought, at least he wasn't letting it cause a panic either inside these walls or outside in the city.

They reached the great mahogany doors that led into the throne room and a young man in deep purple robes held up a thin-boned hand.

"Just a moment, please, Sirs. I will announce you."

Royce cocked an eyebrow at Torus, who snorted and said nothing. The boy opened the door just far enough to squeeze through, and then disappeared from view. A moment later, the door was opened wide from the inside and he bowed low, his robes flowing out around him.

"His Majesty, the One True King, is expecting you."

"I'd hope so," Torus muttered under his breath. "The old fool is the one who sent for us in the first place."

"This old fool," came a booming voice from atop the dais, "still has better hearing than men half his age, young Torus."

Heron Greymalkin, the One True King, was well into his eighth decade. His back was bent and the little hair he had left stood out over his ears like dandelions gone to seed. He slowly made his way down the wide steps from the throne, leaning on his cane for support. He wore breeches and a vest of fine purple velvet, with a thick medallion of gold, the King's Medal, draped around his neck. The necklace was so grand that Royce had a sudden picture of the frail King being crushed under its weight.

Torus went to one knee at the King's approach, and Royce began to follow suit before Greymalkin waved them off impatiently.

"Bowing and scraping isn't my style, boys." The King chuckled, a raspy sound that reminded Royce of sandpaper on a plank. "I have enough sycophants around without adding you fools to the mix."

"Yes, Your Majesty," Torus got back to his feet, looking no more at ease than he had when they first walked in. The King regarded him for a moment and then turned to Royce.

"Good to see you again, Captain. You're well?"

"As well as can be expected, Your Grace."

"Hmpfh. So what's this all about, Torus? Have those mangy dog men really returned?"

"It seems so, Majesty."

The King leaned heavily on his cane, one hand folded over the other. He looked first at Torus, then to Royce, and back again.

"Very well," he sighed. "I suppose we should take this in the council room."

* * *

The enticing call of the city proved to be too much for Tiadaria to withstand. She saw Ecera smile at her as Tia slipped out the side door of the common room and into the alleyway. The sun had just set, painting the western sky with light blues, purples, and pinks. The smell of burning oil was pervasive but not unpleasant. Every hundred feet or so, a lantern hung from a high pole. She marveled a moment, wondering how they managed to light as many lanterns as must be spread all over the city.

The thought was abruptly cut off by a sound she recognized very well. The tinkling of a tambourine somewhere nearby. A beat was struck and a high, pretty female voice carried down the alleyway, bouncing off the fronts of shops and homes that were closing up and darkening for the night.

The alley brought her to the main thoroughfare. To her right, it snaked away out of sight toward the giant maw in the mountainside. The palace lie there and the Captain was no doubt meeting with the King this very moment. To the left, the road led toward the market square they had passed through on their way in. Tiadaria decided, for no reason other than simple ignorance that the music must have been coming from the market square. She turned left.

There was nowhere for her to be and she expected that the Captain wouldn't be back to the room until late, if at all. She probably had at least a couple of hours to explore. By then she would be tired and ready to sleep in the first real bed she'd had in a number of weeks.

"Oy! You!" The shout from behind her made her jump. Her hand reflexively went to her throat, ensuring that the scarf was still knotted there. She turned just as a youngster, a loaf of bread in each hand, sprinted past her, nearly knocking her off balance with his shoulder, as he passed.

His pursuer, the fat man who had shouted, doubled over a short distance from Tia. He was bright red and gasping for breath, beads of sweat popping up over his forehead like droplets on a cold mug of ale. The crimson in his face stood out in stark contrast to the white linen coat he wore. He was dusted head to toe with fine white powder. It was on his breeches, all over his coat, even sprinkled lightly through his hair. Gulping down one last huge breath, he looked up a Tia, who still stood rooted in the spot, staring at him.

"Little bugger got the drop on me," he said. "Well, he probably needed it more than I did. Good evening to you, my Lady."

With a half wave, he turned and walked back toward his shop where a young man with a broom was standing in the doorway. They exchanged words that she couldn't hear and then they disappeared inside. The closing of the door signified the end of the work day. Not only for the bakery, but for everything else on this street, it seemed. There was no one else on the road and Tia suddenly felt very alone.

The girl's voice reached out to her again from the distance, reassurance that she wasn't the only living thing in this city of antiquity. Her first few steps toward the market square were tentative. She still wasn't sure where she was going, but she was relatively certain that she would be able to find her way back to the inn. She began counting the number of buildings and how many turns she made, so that if she got turned around, she would at least be able to get back to her room before the Captain missed her.

Market square was a study in organized chaos. As she neared the cacophony, she found an empty doorway and slipped into it, watching in rapt amazement. The number of people in the square was staggering. The closest she had ever been to a gathering of this size was the few times a year that the clans came together for trading and even then, there were more people crammed into this cleared area of cobblestones than made up all of the clans put together.

The wagons had been shuttered for the night and a large platform at the front of the square had been cleared of boxes, crates, and drums. The girl who was singing looked as if she might have been Tia's age, or a little younger. She was lost, her eyes closed, her head thrown back. Lost in the rapture of the beautiful song that burst from her lips with such intensity that it felt as if Tia might be deafened by the sound as it rolled out across the crowd.

A lanky man sat on the corner of the platform, a large drum between his legs. No slave ship quartermaster had ever kept a beat so relentlessly. To the singer's left, a woman with hair so dark it looked as if the night had wrapped itself around her head; was playing a strange stringed instrument that Tia had never seen. She sat behind its curved back, wrapping her arms around it in an intimate embrace as she plucked at the strings.

Music, like most other things, was utilitarian in the clans. There were saga-songs, stories told to the beat of a drum, but Tiadaria had never heard anything like this. This was music created from passion, not from purpose. It was music that reached deep inside her and clenched at her heart, threatening to wring tears from her eyes. Whatever she had expected to come from her explorations, this hadn't been it. She was a world away from the only home she had ever known. Not only in distance but in custom and attitude as well.

There was a moment of silence and then the crowd erupted in a roaring that Tia could feel through the soles of her boots. Panic flooded through her until she realized that the song had come to an end and these people were showering the performers with their thundering approval. Emboldened by the crowd, Tiadaria lent her voice to the crescendo, pounding her hands together in the most sincere applause she had ever given.

"Beautiful, isn't it?"

The voice in her ear startled her. Not only because of the proximity, but because she hadn't noticed the man's approach. He was leaning over her shoulder, his head covered with a half-helm. Tia nodded, turning to get a better look at him.

He was clad in heavy armor, a black dragon emblazoned on the breastplate. It was a knight's armor and belatedly, Tia realized that the man who had been standing behind her for who knew how long was a city guard, or at the very least, a part of the Grand Army of the Imperium. Tia recognized the sigil. The Captain kept armor in his war chest that bore the same crest. Even his fighting armor, the thin white silk with the fine ringlets of silver, had a black dragon embroidered on the inside breast. A man may leave the army, Tia suspected, but she doubted that the army ever left the man.

Why was he staring at her so? He had been standing just over her shoulder; certainly he had seen through the gauzy material of the scarf and seen that she was a slave. Her collar would have betrayed her and he would lower his pike and march her off through the crowd, and object of their scorn

and ridicule. Tia had heard stories of what happened
to convicts who were paraded through the streets of
whatever town or holding they had committed their
crimes in. Those stories didn't oft end well.

The knight's scrutiny seemed to increase. He
cocked his head at her and then pointed to his ear.

"I said," he nearly shouted over the din,
"Beautiful isn't it?"

Foolish, stupid girl. Tia berated herself as she
smiled at the man, whose face settled into more
relaxed lines.

"Yes," she replied, equally loudly, for the girl
had started a new song, this one much faster than
the last. "Quite!"

The man smiled, patted her on the shoulder,
and worked his way through the crowd. He nodded
to this person and that one, stopping to converse
with others only briefly as he made his rounds. It
wasn't long before he was completely long from
view.

Tia's chest ached and she let out a rush of
breath that made her head swim. She hadn't even
realized she had been holding it. She rubbed the
area under her rib cage, trying to massage the
soreness of the extended effort away. Pairs were
breaking off in the square now, and the crowd
pushed back from the center to allow those who
wished to dance the space to do so, unimpeded.

The outward expansion of the gathering
invaded Tia's secluded doorway. Where she had
been alone a moment before, she was now pressed

among a mass of bodies that ebbed and flowed like the tide. She was assaulted by a number of smells, some of them pleasant, others less so. Her heart began to race and she knew that she needed to get back to the inn, back to relative safety and comfort.

Running on dry sand was easier than moving through the ever-shifting throng of people in her way. It seemed that every time she made a few steps headway toward the inn, she was buffeted backward, to the side, or had to detour around some reveler who, lost in the music, disregarded any attempt for her to slip past expediently. The struggle felt like it went on forever, but she was finally free. She slipped into an alleyway, comforted by the cool blackness there and the relative silence.

Getting her bearings, she was able to deduce that she wasn't too far off from the inn. If this inn met up with a road parallel to the main road, she could cut a few minutes off her trip by following the alley down to its end. Wanting nothing more than to be in the comfort of the inn, in her bed, fast asleep, she decided to risk it.

The alleys were a stark contrast to the well-lit streets. The blackness seemed to engulf her as she walked and she found herself trailing her fingers down the fieldstone wall beside her, a comforting presence that kept her focused and confident that she was still moving in the right direction. The night seemed to lighten ahead, and Tia saw that her alley joined another at right angles. There must be a lantern or oil lamp down the far alley that was shedding pale, butter colored light over the joint where the walls of the pathways met.

Tiadaria had almost reached the pool of light when a robed figure backed into the alley ahead of her. Momentum carried her another few steps before she was able to stop. The robed figure clutched its stomach, the cream-colored robes stained with blood. So much blood. It slipped through the figure's clenched fingers and spattered onto the moss etched stones. Tia felt the hair on the back of her neck stand up and she pulled her belt dagger free, ignoring the now familiar jolt that went up her arm and settled into the base of her spine.

No sooner was the blade free than a massive black shape bounded into the alley. It struck the robed figure in a blur, sending it crashing against the wall. There was a moist thud and the body slid down to a sitting position, its legs sprawled grotesquely outward. Tia shifted into the offensive stance the Captain had taught her, but even as her instinct took over, she felt her stomach clench as the beast turned its full attention on her.

Eyes glowing with blue fire, it snarled, its powerful legs bunching, preparing to spring. There was a scream from the alley behind Tia. Someone, possibly one of the revelers from the square, had stumbled into the alley and found something horribly at odds with the pleasantness of the evening.

The creature's ears swiveled, its fangs glistening with spittle in the dim light of the far off lantern. With a low growl, it leapt off the way it had come, leaving Tia standing there with her blade in her hand and a body at her feet. There were shouts behind her now. She knew that she should sheath the dagger and check on the robed figure laid out before her, but she couldn't seem to make her body obey. Her arm dropped to her side, the dagger clasped lightly in fingers made nerveless by shock.

Someone grabbed her and wheeled her away from the body, pushing her up against the wall. They plucked the dagger from her hand.

"He's dead," someone said. It was a man's voice, flat and devoid of emotion.

"Let me through," someone snarled, and the growing crowd reluctantly parted enough for a man clad in silver armor to squeeze through. He carried a large lantern and it registered somewhere in the back of Tia's mind that it was a street lantern. They took them off the poles. That's obviously how they lit them. It made perfect sense. Another part of her screamed that none of this made sense. That there was no single part of any of this that made any sense at all. She wanted to silence that nagging voice, to tell it to shut up and leave her alone, but it kept nagging at her, like the echo of a pebble dropped down a deep well.

"She stabbed him!" That voice was shrill, a woman's on the verge of hysteria. "I saw it."

"There's no blood," Tia heard herself say. She meant on her dagger. There wouldn't be any blood on the dagger, since she hadn't done anything. A slow thought bubbled up to her. Someone had taken the dagger, she didn't know who.

"There's plenty of blood, you silly bitch." A man's voice, hard and vindictive.

"Silence!" The knight's roar caused the crowd to back up a few steps. He lifted the lantern and shone it directly into Tia's face. She squinted against the light, but recognized him easily. It was the knight she had spoken to in the square. How long ago had that been? It seemed like years. If there was any time for the Captain to appear, as if out of nowhere, like he did...now was that time.

"I know you," the knight said slowly. "I spoke to you earlier this evening."

Tia nodded, feeling bile rise up in the back of her throat. She was determined not to add humiliation to the events of the evening by vomiting all over her boots, or worse, the knight himself. A leaden hand went to her throat, fighting back the wave of nausea that crashed over her, threatening to carry her away.

The gesture was ill-advised. The knight held the lantern closer. A flicker of, something, flashed across his features. So quickly that Tia wasn't sure she even saw it. His thick fingers went to the end of the scarf and tugged it free. The thin fabric unwound itself readily, as if it was eager to give up her darkest secret. As it fell, there was a gasp from the crowd. Her collar stood out in black damnation against her pale skin.

"A slave!"

"Run her through!"

"Take her head!"

"ENOUGH!" The knight bellowed, bringing the butt of his halberd down on the pavers so hard that a few sparks leapt from the bottom of the weapon. "You lot go about your business. There will be no vigilante justice here tonight. Not while I still stand."

He glowered at them, and the crowd began to disperse. In a few moments, the only men standing in the alley were the knight and two men clad in robes identical to that of the corpse. One of them held her dagger. He was turning it over in his hands, holding it toward the light of the knight's lantern.

"There's no blood on this dagger, Valyn." The man tipped the blade toward the knight, showing him the proof. He used the tip of the dagger as a pointer, first at the cobblestones and then at the body. "Plenty of blood on the stones and his robes. You're not going to tell me this dagger struck the blow."

"I'm not going to tell you anything, Faxon." Valyn propped his weapon against the wall and scrubbed at his face with his now free hand. "Now, slave, tell me exactly what happened."

"She has a name, Valyn." Faxon stepped forward, the other robed man a step behind him, a living shadow. "What's your name girl?"

"Tiadaria, Sir."

"Where is your Master, Tiadaria?"

"The Captain had a meeting with Torus in the palace."

Faxon and Valyn exchanged startled glances. It was obvious that whatever answers they had expected from her, this wasn't it.

"The Captain," Valyn muttered, as if he couldn't believe his ears. "You don't think she means--"

"Who else is referred to as The Captain, by practically everyone in the Imperium, Valyn?"

"I don't believe it. Not even for a minute." A flush began to creep up from his neck and colored his cheeks.

"Easy, Valyn." Faxon clapped the man on the shoulder before he turned back to Tia. "Just to be clear, you're saying that your Master is Royce MacDungren? Former Captain of the Grand Army of the Imperium and war hero to the realm?"

Tiadaria nodded.

"Great Gatzbin's gonads," he swore softly. Faxon motioned for his shadow to lift the body. "We need to get to the palace, Valyn. Right now."

~~~~

Chapter 13

Royce MacDungren, Former Captain of the Grand Army of the Imperium and war hero to the realm was furious. White-hot anger boiled just below the surface of his carefully composed and impassive facade. The crier had come racing into the council chamber with news that a slave had murdered a mage. The Lord-Knight of the Guard and Master Faxon were on their way to the palace, he said. He took two breaths fit for a dragon, and then asked his sovereign if his grace cared to return a message. Heron thanked him for his service and dismissed him.

The wizened King turned to Royce and Torus, subjecting them to a scrutiny that would have made lesser men pale. "What do you boys know of this?"

"Nothing, Your Grace." Royce replied quickly, the lie bitter and heavy on his tongue.

"I won't tolerate liars, Royce, not even a man as highly decorated and honorable as you. Your jaw could have cracked walnuts when the crier said slave. So what's going on?"

In for a fraction, in for the crown, Royce thought. Though the recounting was hurried, he ran the King through the events of the last few weeks. He omitted the fact that there were two bodies burned down to ash and bone off the trade road to the far south of King's Reach. There was such a thing as too much honesty. When he had finished, the King shook his head, scratching the wisps of hair over his ears.

"You certainly don't like doing things the simple way, do you Royce?"

Torus snorted. The King eyed him for a moment before he went on.

"Would she have done this?"

"No," Royce replied emphatically, shaking his head. "I don't know what happened out there, but she wouldn't murder someone."

"Not even to keep her secret?" Torus's voice was quiet and measured.

Royce looked at him. The doubt was justified. Slaves were known to go to desperate lengths to keep their status a secret. To keep the shame and indignity at bay for as long as they could. The figures here didn't sum. Royce was positive that whatever had happened, the girl hadn't been the aggressor.

"No." His simple reply held grave weight behind it, and Torus turned away, unable to hold his gaze.

"Enough, you two." The King lowered his rickety frame into a sturdy chair and poured a glass of wine from a flagon on the council table. "We'll get to the bottom of this soon enough."

No sooner was that said than Valyn and Faxon entered with Tiadaria. Another man in a robe followed them. Royce recognized him as Adamon, a mage and Grand Inquisitor of the Academy of Arcane Arts and Sciences.

Royce swallowed hard against the sudden lump in his throat. Inquisitors had one role and one role only: to mete out justice to errant mages. There were many forms that justice could take, but the most severe was censure. The ritual would sever the link between the mage and their magic. In many cases, it was a fate worse than death.

Deprived of their connection to the Quintessential Sphere, the energy of all things, the mages would often go mad. Those that didn't often turned to suicide to end their torment. The few that remained were hollow husks, shells of the men and women they had once been. They were referred to by many as the lost, and Royce couldn't help but agree. There was a difference between living and merely existing.

So why was Adamon here? Had they learned Tiadaria's secret, and by extension, his? Confronted with a reality that countermanded the natural order, had they sought to censure the girl? The talent for using both spell and steel was one that Royce had thought was limited to his bloodline. Tiadaria proved that untrue. How many others in the world had the ability? How long would it take for the Academy to discover their existence and hunt them down?

The Academy had little tolerance for rogue mages, those who didn't receive formal training from childhood and had been overseen in their strict hierarchy. If they had discovered that the girl was a slave as well as a mage...

Valyn dropped to one knee before the King, his salute dismissed by a half-hearted wave from the sovereign. The mages bowed respectfully but did not kneel. Their haughty demeanor had always ruffled Royce's feathers. He wondered if they'd retain their smug and superior airs if he told them that he too, was tapped into the Quintessential Sphere. He reined in his savage thoughts. Bouncing back and forth between fear and hostility was a good way to get killed. He forced himself to breath, struggling to attain an inner calm that matched his passive exterior.

"Alright," the King said, looking each man in the eye in turn. "What's going on?"

The sudden outburst from all sides that resulted from that simple question would have been comical under any other circumstance. Valyn and Faxon both took up their tale at the same time, with Tiadaria chiming in with her own explanation just a moment after. Shaking his head, the King held up his hand for silence.

"If I may," Adamon said quietly, stepping between Faxon and Valyn and approaching the King. "The slave was found in possession of this dagger."

The inquisitor produced the weapon and offered it to the King, hilt first. The King took the offering and turned it over in his hands as Adamon continued.

"An Initiate was murdered tonight, a stone's throw from the market square. I don't know why he was outside the Academy past curfew, but that seems to be going around." He looked at Tia and she dropped her eyes. "I do know that the dagger you now hold did not kill him. The wound was torn, not made by as sharp or fine a blade as that one. The girl, it would seem, is innocent of murder. As for her presence in the city..." He nodded to Royce, who stiffened at the gesture. "Regardless of why she is here, she is, and she is the only witness to what happened in the alley where a promising young mage lost his life."

The King turned the blade over in his hand. Royce wondered how long it would be before he recognized it. Royce had carried that blade every day for nearly thirty years, had stood side by side with the King with it on his belt so often that he had lost track of the occasions and events. Now this girl, a slave, carried it. Certainly he would see the meaning in that, if he chose to see it.

He looked directly into Tiadaria's eyes and she blushed under the shrewd appraisal. They stood that way for several moments, separated by three feet and seventy-odd years. He flipped the blade in the air, as deft as a man less than twice his years, and caught the blade neatly between thumb and forefinger. He offered it to the girl, who hesitated

Martin F. Hengst

only a moment before she accepted the offering and slipped it back into the sheath on her belt.

"What's your name, girl?"

"Tiadaria, Your Grace." She dropped to one knee, a perfect mimic of the gesture that Valyn had made before. Royce dared look at Torus, who no longer seemed to be as openly skeptical of the girl or her role in the killing. His eyes landed on Royce and he shrugged, as if to say it was out of his hands. It was definitely out of their hands, Royce thought. This impromptu performance would play out between Tiadaria and the King. The rest of the players would wait in the wings until their lines were called.

"Lady Tiadaria," the King began with grave formality, "please tell us about the events that transpired tonight."

"Against the Captain's orders, I decided that I wanted to explore the city, so I left the inn and found my way to the market square. There was a girl there singing and a woman playing an instrument as big as she was that I haven't ever seen before. I even saw Sir Valyn making the rounds. After the song was over, the people started dancing and things got very crowded. I was worried about people finding out about me..."

She trailed off and Royce felt for her as her hand went to her neck and touched her collar. If it weren't for that damned collar, things might be different. To her credit, she quickly regained her composure and went on.

"Anyway, I was worried about being discovered, so I decided to go back to the inn. I wanted to get there as quickly as possible, so I figured that the alley that ran between buildings would take me to the road behind the stables. I was almost to the turn between the alleys when the mage backed into the intersection."

"He was already wounded; there was blood all down the front of his robes. Then this...thing, I think it was a Xarundi, threw him into the wall. There was a shout behind me, and that's when Valyn and the others showed up."

"Sir Valyn," the King corrected her absently. "What did the beast look like?"

"It was at least as tall as the mage and it stood up on its feet. I think it had black fur, but I couldn't really see. It had its side turned to me. Before it ran off, it turned on me, and those eyes will stay with me the rest of my life. It's like they were smoldering coals, but blue instead of orange."

Royce watched the startled look that passed between the girl's three warders. Had it been any other time, in any other place, their bewilderment would have been amusing. There wasn't anything funny about this. Not even remotely. Faxon was the first to regain his composure. He grasped Tia's shoulder and turned her toward him.

"You're absolutely certain?"

"Yes, Sir."

"She's telling the truth, Faxon." Torus sighed, running his hand over his close cropped scalp.

"That's why the Captain and I are here. Every living thing in Doshmill was massacred and there were signs of...Well, many of the bodies were desecrated. Then they burned the village to the ground. We think it was a warning."

"A Xarundi...Within the city?"

Royce thought Valyn looked like a man drowning, searching desperately for the end of a rope. In truth, he didn't blame him. The Xarundi had come close to extinguishing mankind once before. The losses the Imperium had taken during the last war were staggering. He shuddered to think of what would happen if the beasts were to attack in force again. There were still those old enough to remember the previous incursion. The panic would be hard to quell.

"Your Grace," Faxon put in quickly, "Adamon and I must return to the Academy immediately. If the Xarundi have returned, or plan to return, we must notify the Head Master tonight. There isn't a moment to waste."

The King nodded. "Agreed. Please bring my regards to Maera. In the meantime, we all need some rest. We're not going to be able to do anything tonight. I believe we should all try to get what sleep we can. Valyn, if you'd be so good as to send a few extra patrols?"

"Yes, Your Grace. Without hesitation."

Valyn saluted and, turning on his heel, stomped off. Faxon and Adamon followed, leaving Tiadaria with Royce, Torus, and the King.

"Royce," the King said quietly. "You've given so much of your life to your King and country that I hesitate to ask you to put your life on the line yet again."

"But you will anyway." Royce smiled.

"Yes." The King seemed his full age now, bent with the years and the weight of the duties he must now delegate.

"It is my honor to serve." Royce crossed his arm over his chest in a soldier's salute.

Torus stepped forward; following Royce's lead, and saluted.

"It is my honor to serve, Your Grace."

Royce was startled, but not really surprised, when Tiadaria stepped forward, her salute as crisp as either of the soldiers.

"It is my honor to serve the One True King." There was a ring of defiance in her voice and Royce wondered what exactly she was rebelling against at this moment. Her capture? Her slavery? The threat to the Imperium? It could be any, all, or something entirely different.

Others would have wilted under the shrewd measuring look that Heron Greymalkin, fourteenth of his line and Sovereign Lord, now leveled on Tiadaria. Royce noted with approval that her gaze never wavered. In fact, the only indication that she was aware of the King's scrutiny came from the tips of her ears, which had started to turn red in embarrassment.

"You are an odd slave, girl." The King waggled a finger at her. "Most slaves have their rightful place beaten into them."

"With respect, Your Grace, my rightful place is at the Captain's right hand. Where he goes, I follow. His field of battle is my training room, his home is my refuge. His honor is repaid by my loyalty."

Heron turned to Royce. "She sounds like you did, when your father was alive. Scant wonder she carries your blade."

"So you noticed."

"Of course I noticed," the King snapped. "I'm old, not daft. But being old means I need my sleep. Get out, the lot of you. Be back at midday for the war council."

* * *

It was well past midnight when they left the castle. The air was cold and Tia was sorry that she no longer had the scarf wrapped around her neck to protect her from the biting chill. Torus had excused himself just beyond the mouth of the cavern, claiming other business he had to attend to before he slept. That left Tia and the Captain to make their way down deserted streets under the black, moonless sky.

They walked in silence for a long time. Had the Captain not been beside her, Tia had to admit that she would have been a little afraid. The stillness of the night and the echo of their footsteps made an eerie sound, as if they were being stalked from every side. In the back of her mind, the beast attacking the young quintessentialist played over and over.

Every time she thought it had passed, it would pop up again. The blood. The sickening wet thud of the body against the wall. Those blue eyes. The eyes would be what stayed with her the longest. If she closed hers, she could still see those blue eyes, burning with malevolent fire.

Tia resolutely put it out of her mind, yet again. She was being sullen and she knew it. She wished that the Captain would just yell at her, scream at her, hit her, do something other than just walking inexorably toward the inn with his lips pressed together in that disapproving frown.

She knew that she had disappointed him. She could feel it, hanging like a veil between them. She hated disappointing him. She hated even more that he wouldn't let her do anything about it. If she bothered to say anything, he'd just nod and carry on as if nothing had happened. It was infuriating.

At length they reached the inn and crossed the deserted common room to the stairs. In short order they were in their room, the door locked behind them. Tiadaria had never been happier to see a bed in her whole life. She felt like she could sleep for a week.

Now the reprimand would come. They were in private and the Captain had no appearances to maintain. Now he would tell her how disappointed

Martin F. Hengst

he was in her, that she didn't follow his orders and ended up in the middle of something that could have gotten her killed. She climbed into bed, kicked off her boots and waited for the harangue to start.

The Captain undressed, folded his clothes neatly and laid them in a pile on the table. He leaned over the glass globe that protected the candle and with a single puff, blew it out. The room was plunged into blackness. No moon hung in the sky to impart any light and the lanterns on the street were all far below the level of their window. Tiadaria heard him get into bed and the rustling of his covers. The room was quiet and still. His breathing grew slower and more regular.

Tiadaria lay there for a long time after he fell asleep. The fact that he couldn't even talk to her wounded her more deeply than the fact that she had disappointed him. It was true that she had disobeyed. There was no getting around that, but hadn't she also provided valuable information to the realm? To the King? Surely the knowledge that there was a Xarundi running around inside the Imperium's capital city was worth something. A tear, born out of anger and frustration, slipped from the corner of her eye. She brushed it away with a knuckle, determined not to wallow. She couldn't control the Captain's silence, but she could control how she reacted to it.

"I'm not angry with you."

With an inarticulate cry, Tiadaria sat bolt upright. She had been certain that he was asleep.

His voice sent her heart thundering in her chest in a reaction that wasn't entirely fright. The silence had lowered again. She tried to feel him across the darkness. Tried to feel what he was feeling, what he needed to say.

"I'm not angry with you," he repeated and Tia heard the waver in his voice. "I was worried for you. I know what the quints do to rogue mages, and I don't want that for you."

"What would they have done, Sir?"

"Censure," he replied, his voice flat. "They'd take away the things that make you, you. That can't happen. I need you. Solendrea needs you."

Tiadaria felt the sudden weight of all his hopes and expectations on her shoulders. Her chest was tight and the darkness was no longer a thin silk shift, it was a smothering blanket that pressed down on her from all sides and threatened to drag her away with it. She wanted to be held, and comforted, and told that everything was going to be alright. That this man who she had come to love wasn't going to leave her and expect her to carry on his legacy.

"It's coming, isn't it," she asked, inwardly begging him to deny it. "The day when I will be the last."

"Yes."

Her fragile composure cracked and she began to sob. Hot tears streamed down her cheeks, burning rivulets of fear and sorrow. He was preparing her for his death, she thought bitterly. His silence, a macabre portent of things to come. Consumed by her grief, she didn't hear him climb out of his bed, or into hers. He wrapped her in his arms, the bond-shock dancing like lightning across their skin. She turned her head into his chest, the weeping swept over her like a wave that threatened to carry her away.

The Captain's hands, far more gentle now than they ever had been, smoothed her hair down. She bristled at the kindness, only too aware that the comfort she received from him now, that she had wanted from him for so long, would be one of the last times he would be able to offer her that comfort. He tightened his grip as he felt her stiffen. She pushed ineffectually at his chest, furious at him for making her care and then leaving her alone. Tia felt his lips brush her forehead. His tenderness was almost unbearable.

"Shhhh now," he whispered in her ear. His hot breath tickling the nape of her neck where she still leaned against him, as much for support as for comfort. Her hands clutched spasmodically at his scarred chest.

All at once, the terrible grief washed out of her, like someone pulling the plug in a tub drain. Left in its wake was sadness so profound that Tia wondered if she would ever be able to be happy again. Slowly, the sobs subsided, but she dared not move. She had waited so long for his touch that she didn't want to break the tenuous bond between them any sooner than she had to.

"I'm sorry," he whispered, his voice hoarse. It was the first, last, and only time Tiadaria ever heard him cry. "I'm sorry that I put all of this on you. You didn't choose to be on the platform that day, and you didn't choose to be what you are. You certainly didn't choose for me to place all of my hope in you."

She reached up, her palm caressing his cheek. It was her turn to offer what comfort she could.

"It's okay," Tiadaria said softly. "I belong to you. I am what you need me to be, and I'm happy that I can be."

"No--"

She silenced his interruption with a finger across his lips. If she were to stand on her own, without him, she would need to learn to take charge. It was time for him to hear what she had to say. Slave she may be, but she was no one's property. She owned herself. Who she honored with her service was her decision and her decision alone.

"You saved me, Captain. When no one else would. When no one else cared. If it weren't for you, I'd have been dead at least twice over. You've given me my life. The least I can do is to gift that life to you. For as long as you have left."

"And what after?"

She shrugged. "What comes after comes after. You've never treated me as property, but I still belong to you. In a way that I will never belong to anyone else. You've given me purpose and trained my talents to meet that purpose. I've given you my service. I think we both got something we needed."

He didn't answer. He didn't need to. Tiadaria gave him a gentle push and he went to his bed. After she heard him settle, she slid under her own covers. She waited until his breath became deep and regular and then she closed her eyes. Sleep came quickly.

~~~~

Chapter 14

The tunnel to the cathedral was pitch black and narrow, with many blind turns that doubled back on themselves. Countless sub-tunnels branched off in all directions. Many leading nowhere but to a dead-end or a shaft that fell deep into the earth. It was said that a man could spend his lifetime exploring those tunnels and never find the entrance to the holiest of the Xarundi holy places. It was probably so. No other living thing on Solendrea could follow the path that Zarfensis now raced down. Even if they could, there were things in the tunnels that wouldn't threaten the Xarundi, but would make short order of any interlopers.

Zarfensis burst out of the tunnel and raced across a natural stone bridge toward the cathedral. The wind was cold and dank, wafting up from the depths of the chasm that surrounded the huge stone building. The windows danced with blue fire, hundreds of eyes peering out at him, awaiting his arrival. Running on all fours was well and good for travel, but it didn't make for a dignified entrance. As he reached the end of the bridge, he stood on his hind legs, his powerful tail counterbalancing the slightly heavier weight of his muscular arms.

Walking the torch lit path to the cathedral, Zarfensis gazed upward. He had known he was destined to be High Priest when he was still just a pup. He remembered vividly coming to the cathedral with his pack. His sire and grand-sire had been priests, but Zarfensis had proven them to be weak and inferior. Advancing through the ranks of the Shadow Assembly with a combination of deception, cruelty, and guile, Zarfensis had taken control of the Xarundi and the lesser species they controlled. His brethren were a great army, a force to be reckoned with, and soon the army of man would be scattered to the corners of the globe. The dark days of the Cleansing would be repaid in full.

This temple was the seat of his power. Its black granite slabs, shot with lines of white, reached high up into the massive subterranean chamber. Torches cast writhing shadows across the doors, two rectangular stone slabs set in the face of the building, each taller than Zarfensis by double. They slowly retracted as he approached, the mechanism rumbling beneath his feet. Striding into the building, he paid no attention to the few bitches and pups in the antechamber. He pushed through the doors that led into the center chamber, with its rows and rows of benches on which his army now perched. They shot to their feet as he entered, their howls brass thunder that bounced off the stone walls.

Bounding up the stairs to the dais, he raised his arms and the crowd fell silent. Even the lesser races, who had been allowed to stand in the back of the chamber to witness their High Priest, stood expectantly quiet.

"A thousand years ago, man all but wiped the Chosen from the face of Solendrea. They rose up against us, their rightful masters, and drank deeply of the blood of our ancestors. Soon, we will make them feel the pain of the Cleansing as it comes to their doors. We will drink of their blood, feast on their flesh, and we will walk in their cities, confined to our underground sanctuary no longer!"

The roar of the assembly shook the building. Zarfensis could feel it through the pads on his feet, a steady, growing vibration that heralded the conflict that would soon explode from the confines of their refuge.

"Tonight, go and spend time with your bitches and pups. Walk the stone halls that you have walked for your lifetimes, for some of you will not return. Those of you, who fall in battle, fall knowing that you have returned Solendrea to our care; that your sacrifice ensures that we will once again reign supreme. Tomorrow, we begin our assault!"

As one, the assembled Chosen rose to their feet and howled a long, dissonant cry that warned their prey of their coming demise. Zarfensis waved his hand in dismissal, and the cathedral began to disgorge the massive number of bodies it held. The exodus was loud and chaotic, but soon the High Priest was left alone in the cathedral. His ears swiveled to and fro, alert for any indication that some wayward subject might have remained behind. There was only silence.

Zarfensis dropped from the dais and crossed to the rectory, sliding the heavy doorway aside with ease and replacing it behind him. He took the short hall to his chambers in two great leaps and landed lightly on his feet in the sparsely furnished room. Sliding a claw into the space between two rocks, he toggled the hidden switch there. A feral smile crossed his elongated face as the false wall moved out of the way and revealed a curving staircase beyond.

The first few steps were taken in total blackness, but as he descended, the bottom of the circular stairs began to glow with a sinister blue-black light. He could feel the pull of the rune, the sickly-sweet power of it, its tendrils reaching out to encircle his mind. The High Priest could feel it trying to press into his thoughts, to twist them with images of macabre death and pestilence and all things foul and unholy. He allowed the images to wash through him, but steeled his mind against the rune taking over.

The rune was their power. It was a physical link to the power of the Quintessential Sphere. The living embodiment of death, disease, and decay. The Xarundi had held this rune, and its power, for a thousand years, since before the time of the Great Cleansing, when men had all but wiped the chosen from the face of the world. Zarfensis and his holiest priests had studied it, learning its ways, learning to keep it at bay enough that they didn't go mad, but were still able to wield the terrible powers it held.

Necromancy, pestilence, and horror were the way of the Dyr. The power of the rune let them call forth the dead and inflict the living with plagues that would literally eat the flesh from their bones. Then, as they died, the Xarundi would take control of their corpses, turning them against the very men they had fought shoulder to shoulder with. The terror that the Xarundi unleashed against the army of man would be unimaginable. They would pay, Zarfensis swore, for every Chosen whose blood had ever been spilled.

He stepped off the stairs and into the tiny chamber that held the rune. He could feel its sickness now, writhing inside him like a snake coiled around its prey. It tried to burrow into his mind, thin ice cold tendrils of hate and fear that pushed relentlessly at his thoughts. How easy, he thought. How easy it would be to let the rune take over, to control his body and his thoughts. Zarfensis growled, doubling his effort to keep the allure of the rune at bay. To give oneself over to the raw power within it was to be lost, forever. It would consume the soul and leave only a rotting, withering husk in its wake. The rune offered incredible power, but the price was damnation.

The High Priest reached out, his claw tracing the embossed symbol on the surface of the rune. He felt the power crawl up his arm, like the legs of a thousand spiders burrowing into his skin and chewing their way toward the base of his spine. The power was intoxicating and Zarfensis threw his head back in sensual pleasure, panting as he fought to keep his identity safe from the grasping claws of the rune. The infusion continued, heightening his senses until he could feel every crease and crack in the stones under his feet. Finally, the insistent pressure of the rune was unbearable, and Zarfensis bounded up the circular stairs, two at a time.

It wasn't until he was in his quarters, with the secret door sealed behind him, that he felt the siren call of the rune slowly begin to fade. It knew it had lost its quarry...this time. It would allow him to take the power he had gathered from it, knowing that he would be back for more. No matter, Zarfensis thought, the power would grant him the victory over the armies of man and then what happened to him didn't matter. The rune could have him and he would be consumed happily.

Zarfensis' nose twitched. There was someone else in the cathedral. He left the rectory and returned to the sanctuary. Xenir, the Warleader, was crouched before the altar, his long snout tucked down into his chest, his tail flaccid, ears limp. It was an uncharacteristic pose for one of the most fearsome warriors that Zarfensis had ever known. So immersed he was in his supplication that he started when the High Priest laid a heavily muscled hand on his shoulder.

"Have you so little faith in me, brother?"

The Warleader unwound from his crouch and got to his hind legs. He stood a full head taller than Zarfensis and his skin was marred with thick scars and patches of missing fur. One milky eye was lost in a mass of scar that traveled from forehead to jaw line. His good eye blazed, piercing the priest like a white hot brand. He reached out and grasped Zarfensis' arm, their forearms pressed together, clawed hands wrapping around elbows

"My faith in you is absolute, Your Holiness." The Warleader gestured at the altar. "I come to the rune's altar because it helps settle me before battle. I've been...restless."

Zarfensis cocked his head to one side, his critical regard ranging over the Warleader's face. Xenir was well-known for his ability to see all the different layers in the Quintessential Sphere. If he was troubled, there was probably a good reason. Zarfensis was sure of their victory, but if the Warleader had seen a portent, it would serve them well to listen.

"You've had a vision?"

The Warleader snarled. It was a sound of impatience and frustration. "Nothing so clear, Your Holiness. I feel...something. I've seen nothing in the swirling eddies of the Sphere, but it feels as if there is something out there. Waiting. Biding its time."

"No indication of what that something might be?"

Xenir tossed his head, his gums pulling back from his teeth in a feral growl. "No Your Holiness, not for lack of trying."

Zarfensis laid his hand on the Warleader's massive shoulder.

"No matter, Warleader. The Dyr will lead us to victory against the armies of man. Your portent will become clear in its time."

Nose flaring, Xenir shook his head slowly. "I can smell your uncertainty, Your Holiness. I have failed you."

"Nonsense," Zarfensis replied with more conviction than he felt. "Your second sight is a warning, nothing more. You need to rest. We march tomorrow."

"Yes, Your Holiness."

Zarfensis watched Xenir until he had left the cathedral. He stood there for a long while after, worrying over the hidden omen and wondering how they could best heed a warning they didn't understand. Finally he retired to his chambers, putting his own advice into practice.

* * *

Motes of dust danced in the shaft of sunlight that fell through the window of the room she shared with the Captain. When she had woken, he was already gone. There was a note on the table instructing her, in no uncertain terms, to stay within the confines of the inn and the courtyard beyond.

Though she wasn't well pleased with the restriction, Tia knew better than to defy him, especially considering how well her last excursion into the city had gone. She contented herself with pacing the length of the room and back again.

Though the wait was infuriating, she had resolved to remain in the room, not even going as far as the common area. It was stubborn of her, but she wanted to prove that she could follow his orders. Still, not knowing where he was or when he would be back was getting to her. She had chewed all the nails off one hand and had started on the other before she heard the door creak open behind her. She turned and watched the Captain enter the room behind her. He carried a long cedar chest in his powerful arms.

As he turned to place it on the table, she saw her name carved into the front, just above the hasp.

"What is this, Sir?"

The Captain stepped out of the way, gesturing to the box. "Something you're going to need a lot in the very near future, I'm afraid." He smiled at her when she hesitated, her hand outstretched tentatively. "Go on, open it."

Conquering her apprehension at the guarded tone of his voice, she went to the table and lifted the lid of the chest. She peered inside and the lid slipped from numb fingers, slamming closed with a loud bang. Left there holding nothing but air, Tiadaria tried to process what she had seen. Then the Captain was by her side, lifting the lid and folding it as far back as the hinges would go.

He lifted out the fine silk tunic, dyed a rich cobalt blue. Over the thin material, thousands of tiny black metal rings joined with each other. A matte black lattice that spread out from the center of the chest, down the three-quarter sleeves, and all the way to the bottom hem.

"I thought," he said quietly. "That the blue would look good on you. It brings out your eyes, little one."

He offered her the tunic and after another moment of trying to pull herself together, she took it from him. Shrugging out of the coarse linen she had been wearing, she slipped into her armor, all sense of modesty forgotten or disregarded. She longed to feel the weight of it on her. It fit perfectly, hugging shoulder and hip and breast, no excess fabric for an enemy to grab hold of, no give in the chain to catch on something. Her fingers danced over the cold metal.

"Is this--?"

The Captain took the dagger from his belt and struck her armor with the broad side of the blade. She felt the metal contract, a tight but not painful constriction across the entire garment. She watched in awe as the metal expanded to its original size.

"Yes," he nodded. "Witchmetal. Highly durable, but not indestructible. It will serve you well."

From the chest he lifted a pair of breeches that were dyed the same deep blue and constructed in much the same fashion. Tiadaria quickly shucked her pants and slipped on the rest of her armor. A pair of boots finished out the ensemble. She twirled, indulging in a moment of sheer girlish delight as she viewed herself in the full length viewing metal attached to the door. The Captain chuckled and reached back into the chest.

"There's more?" Tiadaria asked, astounded.

"Just a bit."

The Captain withdrew a sword belt and pair of scabbards. The supple leather was dyed the same color as her armor, the clasps and hardware silver that danced and sparkled in the sunlight. The scabbards were curved, like his, but the hilts of the weapons that stuck out above them were nothing like any weapon she had ever before seen. The grips were polished to a bright silver shine and were crafted in the likeness of a winged horse, the wings spreading out to form the guard before sweeping back along the hilt. The legs of the beast lie alongside the guard, giving it the appearance of gliding.

He circled her waist with the belt, pulling it tight so the scabbards rested at her hips. He fussed with it a bit and then apparently satisfied, buckled it. "The Pegasus is a noble, honorable, and highly intelligent creature. One that has been gone from Solendrea for hundreds of years. They represent a legacy of swiftness and passion that I now pass on to you. You've learned everything I can teach you, young Tiadaria. Now it's your turn to fly."

The Captain reached into the chest and Tiadaria wondered what could be left. He had already given her so much. Her throat was tight and she was on the verge of tears already. She wasn't sure how much longer she could keep herself together.

Taking an oddly shaped, matte black instrument from the chest, he beckoned her to him. She recognized the device and her heart skipped a beat. It was the same tool that Cerrin had used to lock on her collar.

"I thought the collar was permanent," she asked, puzzled.

"It most cases it is. Faxon happens to be a good friend of mine. He knows quite a lot about the enchantment of witchmetal and the tools used to manipulate it. He invented it, after all."

He fitted the end of the instrument over her collar and she suddenly knew what he intended.

"Sir, wait, please!"

His grip on the tool slackened and he looked at her questioningly. "You're a slave no longer, Tiadaria. You shouldn't wear a collar."

She took his hand in hers and gently removed the device from the band around her neck. She folded his hands over it, and then her hands over his.

"I came to you as a slave, as property, but you never treated me like your property. You trained me, taught me, and you helped me find my purpose.

Everything that I am, or want to be, I learned from you. The collar has never defined me. You showed me how to choose what I wanted for myself. I'd like to keep it. It's a reminder that things happen as they're supposed to...and that freedom can be found in the unlikeliest places."

"It's a tactical liability," he protested. "An enemy could use it against you. A strike against the collar could render you vulnerable at the worst time. Gasping for breath on the battlefield isn't how you want to die."

"No, it's not," she admitted with a wry smile. "We're all vulnerable in our own ways, Captain. This is no better, or worse, than any of them. Please respect my decision. You've taught me well, and I choose to keep the collar to honor the man who made certain that it would never bind me."

"If that's really what you wish." He tossed the instrument back into the chest, looking at her with thinly veiled skepticism.

"It is, Captain."

She threw her arms around him, drawing him close and laying her head against his chest. They stood there for a long time, bathed in the golden sunlight of the rapidly dying day.

~~~~

Chapter 15

Royce and Tiadaria were among the last to enter the council chamber. The vaulted ceilings, each with a painting of some important moment in Solendrea's history, were normally a delight for Royce. Today, however, his mind was elsewhere. Tiadaria had changed. She still wore the collar, which he thought was a distraction at best and a hazard at worst. It had been her decision to keep it and he had to respect her wishes.

Collar or not, she had changed. No longer did she follow behind him. She kept step at his side, a smaller version of the warrior whom she did her best to emulate. Her chin was tipped a little higher, her eyes flashing with the stubborn defiance that Royce had come to know and understand very well. She had become a powerful warrior in her own right, no longer overshadowed by his skill, but a fitting complement to it.

There was a cold ache in his belly that had nothing to do with this council or the battles that they soon would face. Over the past few days, the medicine in his flask had done little to ease the gnawing pain that had grown worse with every morning. He had spied himself in the mirror this morning before they left the inn. He was pale and haggard. Royce thought, with no small amount of remorse, that their departure from the inn would mark the last time he would stay in such an establishment. There were many things that were drawing to a close now.

As they crossed the threshold into the council chamber, all activity stopped. Faxon and Adamon looked up from the table where they had been talking. Torus and his men, gathered around a large map, paused in their strategizing and looked up at them. Even the King, high on his council chair, peered at them as they entered the room. Let them stare, Royce thought. Every one of these men, save the quints, had once followed him into battle. Let them see that he had passed the torch to the spectacular young woman who stood beside him.

Tiadaria was resplendent in her royal blue armor. The witchmetal rings caught no light, but seemed to ripple in waves of shadow across the fine silk. Her weapons hung at her sides, their silver hilts sending motes of reflected lantern light dancing across the floor. If anyone noted the collar, they ignored it.

Torus raised his hand, greeting her as an equal. The mages nodded gravely. The King, leaning on his cane, made his way down the few steps to the floor of the chamber and met them as they crossed the room.

"I'd have thought you would do something about that collar, Royce."

"He attempted to, Your Grace," Tiadaria bowed respectfully from the waist. "I asked to keep it."

"Keep it?" Heron Greymalkin was aghast. "Whatever for?"

"Because it is a solid reminder that one can overcome the worst adversity if one sets their mind to it...and has the right kind of teacher."

The King peered at the girl, then to Royce, then back to the girl. Royce suspected that the King would have still preferred her to be without the collar, but in the end, it wasn't his decision. Tiadaria had decided what was best for her, and Royce wasn't inclined to argue. She was perfectly capable of making her own decisions now. She'd have to. It was time for her to stand on her own and make her own legacy, or die trying. Just as he had.

"Well, young Tiadaria, when this mess is over with, you'll come see me. You'll have a writ signed by my own hand, with my own seal, which states that the collar you wear is by your own choice, not because any man holds dominion over you."

"I'd like that very much, Your Grace."

Royce couldn't help but smile. Stubborn as she was, she was learning diplomacy and tact at a frightening rate. He was sorry that he wouldn't get to see her grow into her new role. He had a feeling that she would surpass even his expectations.

The King grasped her shoulder for a moment, and then called the room to order. They gathered around the map, Royce on one side of the King,

Tiadaria on the other. The quints and the soldiers gathered round. Dragonfell was laid out before them, every road and alley, every twist and turn. Colored markers dotted the surface and Heron wasted no time in pointing some of these out to his council.

"Scouts went out last night and this morning. We have confirmed sightings from some of our best men that the Xarundi are indeed moving on Dragonfell." He pointed to a few of the markers with a crooked finger. "In addition, there is a splinter group that has split off from the main column and has turned toward Blackbeach."

"Gatzbin's gonads!" Faxon swore under his breath. The King looked at him, cocking one bushy eyebrow at his outburst.

"Gatzbin's gonads, indeed." The quint inclined his head in oblique apology and the King went on. "We've released our fastest messengers to Blackbeach. Five of our swiftest coursers are on their way to the Academy even as we speak. We have confidence that the Xarundi won't be able to intercept all five. We've asked for their assistance, after they've dealt with the beasts on their doorstep, of course."

"Your Grace," Adamon put in quietly. "I would like to send my own messenger to the tower, if that's alright?"

The King nodded. "Of course, man. Any help is good help right now." He pointed to a different set of colored markers. "We have defensive troops here, here, and here. They cover all the approaches into the valley. We don't expect them to be able to hold these choke points, so I've issued standing orders that any regiment that gets overrun should fall back behind this line."

The King drew a wide semicircle with his forefinger, indicating an area of crop fields just beyond the edge of the city proper. The regrouping area was far too near the city for Royce's peace of mind, but the valley was relatively small and if they had any chance of keeping the civilians safe, they would need to funnel their attackers away from the innocents and into the waiting arms of the infantry.

Heron tapped the map, looking at each of them in turn.

"This is where you will make your stand, for good or ill. I want the lot of you and your people on this line. You are the last line of defense before those mangy beasts sack Dragonfell and I want you to teach them exactly why they spent the last thousand years hiding in their holes."

"Your will be done," Royce said solemnly.

"As you command," Faxon replied, bowing his head.

"Yes, Your Grace," Torus answered, clicking his heels together and throwing up his hand in a sharp salute.

The King returned the salute, then leaned over the map, indicating the area where they would meet the advancing enemy.

"I don't need to tell you lot what is at stake here." He passed a hand over his face, the weariness of the last few days evident in the lines around his eyes and the dark circles under them. "All of Dragonfell is depending on you. Hell, all the Imperium. That's a tall order to fill, but I have faith in each and every one of you."

There was an uneasy silence, and Royce knew that every individual was reflecting on what was to come. He knew that this would be Tiadaria's first battle, but her face was so pensive and still that he was certain that her thoughts were turned to what would soon be happening outside the city.

"You have about an hour," the King said, breaking the silence. "May all the Gods be with you and watch over you."

With his benediction, they scattered. The mages went in one direction, the soldiers another, Royce and Tiadaria in a third. As they reached the corridor, Royce looked back over his shoulder. The King stood in the center of the empty chamber, leaning on his cane, his head bowed. It pained his heart to see such a noble man disheartened so.

"Come," he said to Tiadaria. "Our destiny waits."

"Yes, Sir."

Royce stopped in his tracks.

"I'm not Sir to you anymore, Tiadaria."

Tia smiled and reached up, laying her gloved hand against his cheek. Her eyes were sad and knowing. His heart skipped a beat at that intimate glance.

"You'll always be Sir to me, Captain. No matter what."

"Then let's go, little one. We have a war to win."

"Yes, Sir."

Though it was the last time Royce left the palace, he did so with lightness in his heart that he had seldom felt before. He knew the battle would be long and tiring, but with Tiadaria fighting at his side, he was sure they would overcome this menace and drive them back into the earth to hide for another millennium.

* * *

The attacking wave of Xarundi warriors spilled through the pass like a swarm of locust. There were so many of them, so close together, that Tiadaria thought it looked like a black, rolling fog was descending into the valley.

The defending lines at the choke points had been turned almost as soon as the two armies met. The soldiers pushed back as much as they could, suffering heavy losses in the face of so many enemies. In the end, they had been routed and forced back to the rendezvous point with the bulk of the Imperium's army.

They returned to the main group just ahead of the mass of Xarundi that were chasing close on their heels. Line commanders ordered the returning troops behind the line to rest and resupply. They would be needed later in the battle to replace their fallen comrades.

As the Xarundi ranks closed, some of the more zealous archers brought their weapons to the ready and Torus shouted out orders for them to hold their fire. Their enemy would need to be much nearer and the bowmen would need to make every shot count. There were a finite number of arrows and seemingly no end to the mass of bodies that raced toward them.

A long, ragged howl went up from the attackers as they raced toward the city. They came on in a crouch, all four powerful limbs propelling them forward with unbelievable speed. The archers loosed the first volley of arrows and they fell on the Xarundi in a deadly rain. Many of the beasts leapt out of the way of the incoming projectiles, in some cases coming up completely off the ground and executing intricate maneuvers to avoid being skewered.

More arrows were fitted to bow strings. Tiadaria could see the burning blue luminescence of their eyes now, tiny points of light that glittered and flashed in the gathering twilight. She drew her swords, relishing in the once painful shock that reminded her of her unique bond to the Quintessential Sphere. She heard the twang of bowstrings and looked past the physical realm, into the one beyond. Sphere-sight showed her each arrow, a streak of light piercing the blackness that massed before her. Where the arrows struck true, there would be a brilliant flash of white that replaced the black shape. Too many of the white streaks were fading out as they fell, their targets unscathed by the airborne fury.

Up and down their ranks, their fighters burned gray or brilliant white. The Captain shone the brightest of them all, a dazzling presence that seemed to pulse with intensity. He stood atop a hastily constructed barricade, his scimitars tracing lazy figure eights. She shifted her sight back to the realm of the living. Their part of the battle would start soon. The first line of Xarundi was almost upon them.

There was a roar from the flanks as the quints unleashed their spells. Magic missiles, white and glowing, streaked across the battlefield, exploding into showers of light when they hit their targets. Balls of flame, shards of ice, and all other manner of magical projectiles slammed into the Xarundi ranks. The beasts were beginning to reply in kind. Small darts fired from their blowguns zipped through the air like angry wasps.

The soldier immediately to Tiadaria's right was hit in the throat. He spun off the barrier, his sword dropping from lifeless fingers. The Xarundi shamans were reanimating their dead, sending the corpses of their fallen brethren shambling into battle for them.

The archers riddled them with arrows, but they continued on their inexorable course toward the humans. A cluster of the undead beasts had nearly reached the far right flank of the defending forces when one of the two cannons on the battlefield roared to life.

The canister shot loaded into the large gun exploded outward in a cone of devastation. The undead Xarundi were torn asunder and the human warriors roared with approval. With the Xarundi ranks weakened, Torus ordered the right lines to attack.

Archers called for resupply, but were met with answering shouts that ammo supplies were critically low. The Captain bellowed for the archers to withdraw and they climbed down off the platforms. The front lines were nearly on each other now. At the Captain's command, the assembled soldiers drew their weapons. The sound of ringing metal echoed up and down the line as blades were drawn from their scabbards. Tiadaria spun her scimitars back and forth, testing their balance and her range.

Faxon called retreat for the quints. The mages would fall back and reassemble to offer what support they could, but their offensive powers were limited by the close quarters the battle would take. There was too much of a risk of hitting their own people accidentally. The armies met, steel clashing against claw.

Tiadaria slipped into sphere-sight and ran for the edge of the platform. At the end, she leapt into the air, tumbling head over heels, out over the front lines and down into the mass of Xarundi warriors. Her arms flashed out as she fell, one blade slicing easily through a skull, the other severing a spine below the ribs. Her dance was as graceful as it was deadly. To her eyes, masses of black vanished in pulses of brilliant white light. Darkness had fallen in the physical realm, the soldiers struggling to hold the line in the black.

The cannon on the left flank lit the night, throwing the shapes of their attackers into start relief against the flash. The cannons were impressive, Tiadaria thought, but they were too slow to load and ready for firing. By the time the great guns were ready, she'd have sliced her way through a score of Xarundi bodies.

Brilliant luminescent globes appeared above the battlefield, and Tiadaria shifted her focus long enough to see that they were just as bright in the real world as they were in the sphere. The quints had summoned miniature suns and set them blazing above the warzone. The humans quickly recovered from the sudden blindness and pressed their enemies back.

Tiadaria spun and whirled, her blades seeking out the center of her attackers, trying to make each strike a lethal one. Claws raked down her arm, the searing pain knocking her out of her commune with the sphere. She spun on her heel and lopped off the head of the creature that wounded her.

She fell back behind a knot of soldiers to assess her wounds. They were long and bleeding freely, but they were shallow. She could wait to dress them until after the battle. A medic was already wading through the sea of bodies to reach her, but she waved him off and once again slipped into chaos.

The Captain was far off to her left, flowing through the tide of Xarundi bodies as effortlessly as she had just moments before. He was covered in blood. It was sprayed across his face like war paint. Tiadaria touched her cheek and found that she was covered in it as well. There was no time to think about how many enemies she had killed to be coated with that much blood. The Xarundi were pressing their attack and she had to defend.

Shifting, she launched herself back into the fray. Later, when she thought about that night, Tiadaria wouldn't be able to say how long she had fought or how many Xarundi she had slain. She only knew that as the battle ground toward its end, that the battlefield was thick with the dead and dying from both sides and that it was difficult to walk on the blood-slicked grass.

* * *

As they loped toward the human city, Xenir and Zarfensis growled orders to the Chosen, ensuring that each pack knew their objective and their assigned targets.

It wasn't long at all before the opposing forces were locked in combat. Darters remained behind the frontline warriors, sending their poisoned projectiles into the human army and roaring with pleasure as the vermin dropped from their barricades.

For each Xarundi that fell, there was a shaman waiting to reanimate the corpse. Those Chosen who had failed and fallen in battle would regain their honor in becoming the automatons that would fight without fear of death or injury for their still living brethren.

As combat raged around them, Xenir and Zarfensis met in the center of the battlefield.

"There! That one!" Zarfensis pointed with a long claw to the human warrior clad in his unique armor. Xenir nodded his agreement.

"And there!" The Warleader said, motioning to the impressive bulk of the leader of the vermin's army. "Cut the head from the viper and the rest will wither and die."

They clasped forearms, a brief gesture of support, and then they were gone. As Zarfensis and Xenir moved through the writhing bodies of the Chosen, several of the warriors broke off from their packs to protect their leaders.

The fighting nearest the city was the most intense, with the Chosen tearing into the vermin with claw and fang. Zarfensis relished in the savagery of it all. Not only would they grind the vermin under their heel, they would drive them from their city as well.

As if granted a boon from the old gods, a momentary lull in the fighting opened a clear path between Zarfensis and the human warrior.

Without hesitation, the High Priest raced forward, claws extended to their furthest reach. He collided with the warrior without checking his speed. They flew, entwined together, into a mass of scurrying vermin who scattered, running away from the conflict.

Zarfensis realized, nearly too late, that this human warrior was different. He was stronger and faster than ordinary vermin and he stank of disease. The smell of corruption filled Zarfensis's nostrils as they fought.

The High Priest was forced to admit that the human warrior was almost his equal in skill. Claw rang against blade as both of them drew on the power of the sphere to grant them any advantage.

Their battle went on for what felt like an eternity. Strike, counterstrike. Feint, counter-feint. The human warrior swung wide, a blow meant to decapitate. With a burst of speed, Zarfensis drove his claws deep into his surprised opponent and lifted him over his head.

He called to the Chosen, wanting to share his victory, but no answering call came. He glanced to his left, but Xenir was nowhere to be seen. The other Xarundi were falling back, driven into retreat by the human mages who had returned to the battlefield as bodies had thinned.

Zarfensis drew his free hand back, determined to sever the vermin's head from his shoulders. His world exploded, throwing him backward. The High Priest landed hard, his leg cracking and buckling under his weight. He plunged into darkness.

* * *

The tide of the battle had turned. The Xarundi were in retreat, the human soldiers and quintessentialists giving chase across the field. As Tiadaria prepared to follow, a searing pain shot through her head and she dropped to her knees, her weapons slipping from her hands. A soldier behind her decapitated a straggling beast-man as it fell toward her, its claws extended.

The beast crumpled and Tia struggled to stand, fighting against a wave of nausea so powerful that it threatened to overwhelm her. At first, she thought the collar had been the cause of the sudden pain, but looking across the field, she saw a massive Xarundi warrior, half again as tall as the others. The beast held the Captain aloft, his long talons protruding from the Captains back, glistening with blood.

The creature raised its other arm to strike at the Captain, but it never got the chance. Spells from Faxon and Adamon slammed into the beast, spinning it into the air and away from the Captain, who fell in a crumpled heap to the ground.

Leaving her swords where they lay, Tiadaria raced toward him, vaulting over bodies and dodging still living warriors as they came between her and her only goal. She ran for what seemed like hours, but finally she reached him.

The Captain's armor was marred by huge gashes, the metal rings broken around the ragged edges of wounds that went all the way through his body. His lower half was slick with blood, the same blood that trickled from his nose and bubbled at the corner of his mouth. Tiadaria called for a cleric, but she knew in her heart that there was no magic powerful enough to save him. His eyes rolled, showing far too much white and she grabbed his head, crushing him to her chest as if she could take his entire essence into her.

"You..." He coughed, blood and spittle flying from his lips. His breaths came in long, wet rattling gasps. "Made me proud. Little one."

"Oh Sir," Tiadaria sobbed, tears etching tiny pale paths through the blood spattered on her face. "Please don't leave me, I need you."

He shook his head slightly, closing his eyes. For a moment, Tiadaria was sure that he had gone. Then he opened his eyes and looked at her, saw her, with total clarity.

"You'll always have me in your heart, little one." His voice was strong, and clear, an echo of the brass thunder that had called the warriors to arms just a few hours before. He raised his hand to caress her cheek, and then he was gone. The tension went out of his body and he was still.

Tiadaria held him that way for a long time. Finally, she reached up and brushed his eyes closed with the tips of her fingers, closing the eyes that had seen so much and told her even more. It wasn't for another few moments that she realized that her sobbing was the only sound she could hear. Looking up, she saw faces around her she recognized. Torus and Faxon, Adamon, the soldiers she had fought beside. Valyn stood there, a bloody graze across his forehead, his armor much dented, pierced by claw, and burnt by spell. They were ranged around her in a wide circle; sword and staff plunged into the earth.

In that simple accord, all of them standing as one, in unison, they honored their fallen hero. For the Captain had been a hero to all of them, on the battlefield and off, for as long as any of them could remember. Their vigil touched her in a way that no words ever would. Her throat was so tight she couldn't speak. The men bowed their heads even as a pathway opened up through the ranks.

Heron Greymalkin, stooped over his cane, made his way slowly into the middle of the circle where the Captain's body lay. He dropped to his knees beside Tiadaria and took her hand in his. Then he wept.

~~~~

Chapter 16

The morning outside her room was cold and gray. It matched the numbness that she felt. Tiadaria had stayed in the palace after the battle, given a fine room with a deep, plush bed. The curtains were velvet and royal purple. The rugs were expertly woven and soft on her bare feet. It was a spectacularly beautiful room and it would have made her very happy if she had been able to experience it.

Instead, she stood at the window and peered out from the open maw of the cavern, across the city. The battlefield was hidden from view by a hundred different intervening buildings, but she could feel it. That was where the Captain had died, where she had held him for the last time. Where her heart had broken. It had only been two days ago, but it felt like two years. They would put his body in the ground today, the last remnant of the legacy of the great man he had been.

There was a light rapping at the door, but she ignored it. She didn't want to see anyone and she certainly didn't want to talk to anyone. It seemed like all she had left to offer anyone who came calling were tears and bitterness. There was another rap at the door. Still she didn't move. She stood there, standing, staring, her eyes straining as if she could see through the buildings to the spot where he had died.

Tiadaria heard the door open and whirled; ready to demand that she be left alone. It was Faxon who entered, his chestnut brown beard a stark contrast to his pale skin and cream-colored robes. He looked as tired and drawn as she felt. She couldn't even muster the strength to cast him out, so instead she turned back to the window. He closed the door softly and came to stand beside her.

They stood together in silence for a long time. Tiadaria had almost forgotten he was there when he spoke.

"I have something for you. Something that Royce asked me to keep for him, just in case something happened to him. He wanted you to have it."

Faxon reached into his robes and produced a folded parcel, the deep blue wax embossed with the Captain's personal seal. Tia took it from him and went to the bed. The mage settled himself in the chair by the window, looking out at the dismal sky spread low over the city. Her fingers trembled as she broke the seal, unfolding the sheaf of papers. As she did so, something fell out of the stack and landed between her feet on the bed. It was the curious little cottage key on its length of black ribbon. She read the letter.

Tiadaria--

Little one, if you're reading this letter, it means that I've fallen. Either to sickness or in battle. I'm sorry that I won't be around to witness you becoming the powerful warrior I know you will be, but it pleases me to have been the instrument that guided you on your path to destiny.

You are now the last swordmage. Faxon is the only person who I trusted to know my secret. Now he knows yours. If you have questions about your powers or abilities, he can be trusted. Trust no one else. He alone will bear the burden that comes with knowledge of our unique gift.

I hope by now you've found the key. The cottage and all my possessions are yours now. The deed to my land is enclosed. Use them as you see fit. Start a new life for yourself. A good life. A happy life.

Try not to mourn overlong, little one. I knew my time was short when I met you, but oh the joy you brought to my last days. I was a better man for having known you.

--Sir

Tiadaria traced the looping scrawl with her finger. Reading the short letter a second time and then a third. Finally, she carefully refolded the parcel and laid it on the bedside table, placing the cottage key reverently on top of it.

"He never spoke of anyone the same way he spoke of you, Tiadaria." Faxon said from his seat by the window. "He'd known he was dying for a long time. You gave him a sense of purpose and a reason to see this last battle through. You saved him."

He chuckled, glancing at her.

"Hell, girl, you probably saved all of us. Without the two of you on the battlefield, things would have ended much differently. We might have won, but at what cost?"

"The Captain said I could trust you...with my...secret."

"Did he?" Faxon raised his eyebrows waggishly. "He probably also warned you about telling anyone else. Heed that advice. The Academy of Arcane Arts and Sciences exists in black and white. There is good, there is bad, there is no middle ground. The untrained are not to wield magic of any kind, those that do face censure or death. Most mages would rather die than face censure, so it's often the same thing."

"Then why do you keep our secret?"

"Because the world doesn't operate in black and white. There are a thousand shades of gray between good and bad, righteous and evil. As a man, I recognize this. I'm nothing if not a pragmatist."

"So you're hedging your bets," Tiadaria said bitterly.

"Not exactly." Faxon shrugged. "I believe in the right tool for the right job, regardless of how that tool came to be, or how it's used. There are many who believe that magic in the hands of the uninitiated is the gravest danger we face."

"Do you?"

"Obviously not. We wouldn't be having this conversation if I did." Faxon steepled his fingers under his chin and stared at her a moment before continuing. "I believe the gravest danger we face is ignorance. You saw what happened out there. How many people would have honestly believed that the Xarundi had returned before they had seen it with their own eyes? Had their own blood spilled?"

"Not many."

"Precious few," Faxon snorted. "You and I...Torus, the Captain...even the King to some extent...we are breeds apart. We don't see the world how we want it to be. We see it how it is."

"For all the good that does us."

The mage spread his hands in an expansive gesture, encompassing the palace and everything beyond.

"We're here. Good triumphed over evil. The realm was spared. We live to fight another day. It is because of us that the rest of the world can live in blissful ignorance. That they can sleep at night without fear of the demon lurking in the dark. We live on to serve."

"Most of us."

Faxon waved a finger at her.

"Your bitterness does you no credit, girl. Royce knew he was dying before he set foot on the battlefield. If you honor him half as much as you claim, you know in your heart that dying in bed wasn't his way. He died with a blade in his hand. There is no finer way for a warrior to die. Don't sully his sacrifice because you're wallowing in pity."

As much as it hurt her to hear it, she knew in her heart that there was no place the Captain would have rather been than on the battlefield, defending the realm and the people who he had dedicated his life to protecting. If she disparaged the manner of his death, she also dismissed the man, and the Captain was more deserving of respect and honor than anyone she had ever known.

"You're right," she chuckled ruefully. "He'd slap me with the broad side of his sword if he knew I was acting this way."

Faxon rose, his heavy robes swirling around his feet like an ebbing tide. He walked to her and took her shoulder in his hand, a gesture not unlike that of the Captain.

"Don't be afraid to mourn," he said softly. "We all miss him and likely will for the rest of our days. Just don't allow your mourning to consume you."

"You'll be there tonight?" she asked, almost plaintively. "For the interment?"

"Of course. We'll all be there."

With that, he left her, sweeping out of the door as quickly as he had entered, leaving her to her thoughts and to the memory of a man who had been more her father than the man she had known from childhood.

* * *

The infection spreading through his left leg smelled like death and decay. The most powerful magic at his disposal had done little to stem the spread of the disease. Zarfensis was cold with more than the chill of night. His body was afire with its attempts to burn off the sickness.

He had cut through the elven lands on his way back to the Warrens, but he was in no condition to fight. Every patrol meant hiding, biding his time, waiting until the cousins of vermin had traveled far enough beyond that he could evade them, even in his current condition. That meant many days spent hiding in caves and outcroppings, one eye and ear wary for any danger while he tried to catch sleep where and when he could.

The night was reserved for travel, when his augmented vision would give him the advantage over nearly every other creature on Solendrea. Now he was nearing the entrance to the labyrinth of tunnels that would lead him into the Warrens and to his salvation. The descent into the earth took an agonizingly long time, but eventually, he slipped past the last fissure into the cathedral hall.

The Warrens were in chaos. All around the cathedral chamber lay dead and dying chosen. Clerics and shaman dashed to and fro, trying to ease the suffering of the injured, or offer a quick death to those too far gone to recover. The sheer number of wounded underlined how badly they had been routed. Their losses were staggering.

Zarfensis sighed with relief as he saw a familiar hulk lope out of the cathedral. Xenir, then, had survived. Perhaps his second sight had spared him from the worse ravages of battle. The High Priest limped toward the massive Warleader, who had stopped to offer comfort to some of the injured. He felt the weight of many eyes on him as he passed. He knew that many of the Chosen would blame him for this failure. He wondered how many of the Chosen had known that Xenir had predicted their defeat.

"Your Holiness!" Xenir bounded to Zarfensis, offering him a shoulder as the High Priest stumbled. "You are injured!"

The Warleader howled and a Xarundi in cleric's robes bounded over to them. The Warleader and the cleric escorted him inside the cathedral and onto a stone bench. As the cleric inspected his wounds, Zarfensis spoke to Xenir.

"It would seem that your feeling was well founded, Xenir."

The Warleader bowed his head and Zarfensis reached out and laid a hand on his arm.

"The fault does not lie with you, Xenir. I was the one who made the decision. I was the one who pressed the attack. Any blame for this, if there is blame, is mine to hold."

"There will be blame," the Warleader said sadly. "I was on my way to find you when we met. I was sent to bring you to the Assembly."

Zarfensis experienced a sudden chill that had nothing to do with fever. The Warleader hadn't said the pack council, which was the ruling body of the Chosen. He had said the Assembly. He licked his muzzle, a nervous habit he had acquired as a pup. It wasn't lost on the Warleader, who nodded.

"Yes, Your Holiness. The rest of the Seven are here."

"When did they arrive?"

"The last of them arrived this morning."

"I see." Zarfensis dismissed the cleric with a flick of his claws. "Be gone, sister. No cleric can save me now."

The Warleader shifted, his unease palpable. "Allow me to walk with you, Your Holiness?"

Zarfensis shook his head.

"Not this time, my brother. Where I must go, you cannot follow."

* * *

The coach wound its way down the narrow path that led to the cottage. It felt like a lifetime since she had last been here. After the battle, she hadn't wanted to leave Dragonfell. It was irrational, she knew, but somehow, it felt as if leaving the place where the Captain would lay for eternity, she was abandoning him somehow. She felt a special kinship with the city and its people.

Tiadaria had passed the winter in the city, splitting her time in residence between the palace and Ecera's inn. She had taken the time to explore the city and learn the history of the land from its vast libraries, its people, and even from the King. They had needed each other, those first few weeks. The Captain had been like a son to him, and a father to her. Together they had weathered the worst of their grief, coming into spring with a renewed appreciation for life and vigor. Though it was hard for her to say goodbye, she also knew it was necessary. Staying in Dragonfell meant living in the past and that was something she just couldn't do.

Torus reigned in the horses and turned in his seat to face her. The battle and his loss had weighed heavily on him. The creases around his eyes were deeper and the eyes themselves were sadder. Still, he managed a smile for her.

"I could stay," he offered tentatively. "You know, for a while. To get you settled."

Tia laid her hand on his cheek, returning the smile.

"Thank you, Torus." She patted his cheek gently, and then folded her hands around the letter that lay in her lap. "But that won't be necessary. This is the only place that's ever really been home."

The mammoth man looked out over her shoulder and nodded. He swallowed hard. Tia looked down into her lap. Tears seemed to come much easier for all of them, these days. Clutching the worn letter in her hand, she dropped from the coach and went to the gate. The hinges were rusty and squawked in protest as she pushed it open. They would need to be oiled. There were probably a hundred little things that needed to be put back in order.

The little yard was littered with the debris of a full and harsh winter, but here and there the bulbous heads of flowers were beginning to poke through the ground. It would be summer soon, and all would be light and warmth. The gutters were choked with leaves and there were tufts of brown grass sticking up through the cobblestones. There was work to do here definitely, but it would feel good to set things right. The cottage was hers now. She had the deed in her hand and a letter, signed by the King, which named her as the Captain's legal heir and successor.

Torus brought her trunk from the coach and sat it on the path near the door. She could tell it wasn't comfortable for him to be here. He shifted from one foot to the other, peering around the little yard, looking anywhere but directly at her. How long, she wondered. How long would his ghost linger for all of them?

"Well," he finally said, clearing his throat. "I guess this is it then."

She nodded.

"I suppose it is."

They stood in silence for a moment. Somewhere in the distance, a songbird whistled out its beautiful tune. The air was warm and thick with the smell of life and fresh grass. They stood, listening in silence, until the song faded into the distance. Torus cleared his throat, filling the space between them.

"I'll see you around, Tiadaria." His voice cracked as he turned toward the coach. "If you're ever in Dragonfell..."

Tiadaria stepped up to him, wrapping her arms as far around his massive frame as she could reach. He patted her back with a gloved hand, as if he was afraid she was going to break apart. It was an awkward gesture, but one she appreciated all the same.

"Thank you, Torus," she said into his chest. "Thank you for everything. I'll come and see you soon, okay?"

"I'd like that," he said, nodding. "I'd like that very much."

He made his way back to the coach with jerky steps and climbed to the driver's seat. He gave her a curt wave, flicked the reins, and was gone. Tia ran to the gate and into the road, watching the coach draw away until it turned onto the trade road and was gone. The cottage was quiet and still, save for the murmurings of the insects and birds.

Tiadaria was alone for the first time in months. Her fingers went to her collar, as they often did now when she was upset or nervous, tracing the smooth cool metal around the base of her neck. She missed the Captain so much that her heart ached almost constantly. There was an empty place where he had been and she wasn't sure that place would ever be adequately filled ever again. The crushing pain of his loss, however, had passed. She could think about their time together without wanting to curl up and cry.

Walking to the door to the cottage, she fished out a tiny brass key from inside her tunic. Its length of black ribbon was worn, but the myriad array of gears, nubs, and depressions shone as brightly as ever. She slid the key into the lock and listened as the mechanism whirred and ground, clicked and tinkled. The latch gave and the door opened with a faint click.

Tiadaria was home.

# # #

THE ADVENTURE CONTINUES IN:
The Darkest Hour

A thin green tendril snaked upward out of the earth. It slithered toward its prey, silent and unnoticed. The constriction started as a gentle squeeze, increasing rapidly as it took hold, threatening to choke the life out of its chosen victim.

Tiadaria grasped the weed just above the root and yanked it out of the ground. She shook the dirt from the bundle before tossing it over her shoulder into a growing pile on the cobblestone pathway. Spring had come to the Imperium and already birds were singing in the trees at the edge of the fence that circled the cottage.

Winter had been cold and dark, with the loss of the Captain being harder to bear during the bleakness of the frozen months.

Still, with time, the sharp pain of loss had been reduced to a dull ache. Two years had passed since that fateful night on the battlefield outside of Dragonfell. The events of that night had forever changed her, but as that first winter had changed into spring, she found the loss easier to bear than she would have imagined. The time she spent in Dragonfell after his death had helped immensely.

This past winter had been easier still. She supposed it was true; time heals all wounds.

She still felt the Captain's presence in a very real way around the cottage. Although she was frequently called to Blackbeach or Dragonfell on Imperium business, she had no desire to live anywhere but King's Reach or the little home she had inherited from her former mentor. A new constable and magistrate kept things quiet in the tiny hamlet and it was a welcome respite from the constant flurry of activity in the capital.

There was a creak from the end of the path and Tiadaria was instantly alert. The gate hinge was left unoiled for precisely that reason. It was an innocuous warning, a first line of defense against anyone who might seek to sneak up on her. True, they could just jump the fence, but even King's Reach, so far from the heart of the Imperium, was mostly civilized.

The man who stood at the end of the path was tall and lanky. His curly brown hair peeked out from under the wide-brimmed hat he wore pulled down over his eyes, casting a shadow over his face. He wore a dirt-stained coverall and was stooped over, a common posture ailment for those who walked behind the plow. His dirty hands also lent credence to the image, but the little hairs on the back of her neck stood on end. Something told her this was no simple farmer. She shifted into sphere-sight. It was second nature now. She cast out toward the man standing at the end of her path and inspected him in minute detail.

"I didn't mean to startle you, Lady Tiadaria," he said in a soft voice, very much at odds with his appearance. "I assure you that I am no threat to you. However, I suspect you've already allayed yourself of that worry."

Tiadaria shifted her sight back to the physical realm. Her cool blue eyes ranged over him as she pushed herself to her knees, then to her feet. She brushed her palms against the thighs of her breeches, loosening the worst of the dirt that was caked on her hands. Her visitor didn't seem concerned by her dirty attire and unkempt hair. The latter she twisted into a crude blond knot at the base of her neck.

"I don't believe we've met…" She trailed off, silently prompting him for a name, since none had been offered.

"Cabot, Lady Tiadaria, with the Imperium Intelligence Service." He glanced around and nodded to himself as if satisfied. "Do you think we could speak? Inside?"

Tiadaria led him into the little cottage, stopping only to fit a tiny brass key into the complicated lock set in the door. Cabot's eyes widened slightly as the lock made its customary series of pops, snaps, and twangs before the key, turning on its own accord, unlocked the door. She pushed it open and gestured for Cabot to precede her into the common room.

"To what do I owe the honor of a visit by Imperium Intelligence, Cabot?" she asked, ushering him onto a stool by the long trestle table. There were neat stacks of parchment at the end of the table and the far wall had a myriad of maps pinned to it. Weapons and armor of all types hung from pegs around the room. Cabot's awestruck expression was almost comical, but Tiadaria could forgive him that. It was an impressive room. It had been so when it was the Captain's and it remained so under her care.

"My Lady—"

"Tia is fine, Cabot." She felt a little silly correcting someone several years her elder, but as he had made no attempt to drop the title, she did it for him.

"Tia then," he said, inclining his head in thanks. "Master Faxon Indra at the Academy of Arcane Arts and Sciences sent me to you. He says it is of vital importance for you to have my full report. Since I'm on my way back out on assignment, Master Faxon asked me to visit you."

If Faxon had sent Cabot to her, there must be something foul afoot. There was a standing joke between Tia and the quintessentialist that the only time Faxon summoned her to Blackbeach was when something horrible was about to happen. Or already in progress. She sighed.

"Alright then," she said, slipping onto a stool and leaning forward over the table. "You'd better tell me all of it."

"I'm afraid all of it isn't very much." Cabot spread his hands in a gesture of apology. "All we have to go on are rumors and hearsay. The Xarundi have apparently been licking their wounds and they are striking out again, attacking some of the smaller human settlements nearest to the Warrens. We know that they were badly fragmented after the battle at Dragonfell. We have a mole within the Shadow Assembly—"

"Really?"

"Yes, Lady...I mean, Tia. We have several moles that have infiltrated the lower ranks of the Assembly. Most of them report to lower functionaries, which is part of the problem. There is talk that one of their seers has had a vision of a great and powerful artifact. Others dismiss this as rumor and misdirection. Either way, we don't know what the artifact is, or where it might be."

"But if the Xarundi are seeking it out, there's a good chance that it doesn't bode well for the Imperium. Or me."

"Exactly. So Faxon—"

"Wants me to get near enough the Warrens to see what's going on and what we can do to stop it," she finished for him. Cabot slowly shook his head.

"No, not exactly. He wants you to meet with him in Blackbeach so the two of you can go through the Great Library and see if there are any clues as to what the artifact might be and where the Xarundi could be looking for it."

"Ugh," Tiadaria groaned. "Research. What is it with quints and their research? I'll take a blade in my hand over a book any day."

Cabot smiled tolerantly. "I'm not inclined to disagree with you, Lady Tia."

"If that's all then?" Tiadaria pushed off the table and got to her feet, extending her hand to Cabot as he did the same. He grasped it tightly and smiled.

"I have nothing more," he said. "It was nice to meet the heroine of Dragonfell in person, though. Not very often that a man gets to say that he was in the presence of greatness."

"Oh stop it," Tiadaria snapped, her cheeks burning red. "There were many on that battlefield that night."

"True." Cabot nodded. "But not many who laid out two score of Xarundi before the rest of us could find our daggers."

"You were there?" She asked, touching his shoulder lightly.

"Aye, Lady." He sighed. "A shame about the Captain, but he wouldn't have wanted it any other way. May we all be so lucky when our time comes."

"Indeed." Tiadaria's throat was tight, her chest aching.

Cabot seemed to shrug off his melancholy.

"Anyway, it was nice to meet you, My Lady. I'll see myself out."

Tiadaria stared after him long after he had slipped out through the exquisite door. She went to the window and watched him take the path away from the cottage with long strides, his farmer affectation a memory.

Cabot's innocent remark had stung her in a tender place. How long, she wondered, would old ghosts continue to haunt her?

Continue the adventure in The Darkest Hour, available now on Amazon.com.

If you enjoyed this book, please take a moment and review it favorably.

Thank you.

# # #

ABOUT THE AUTHOR

Martin F. Hengst resides in South Central Pennsylvania with his wife and two children.

An avid reader since childhood, he attributes his love for fantasy and science fiction to his father. Martin's passion is creating intricate stories with intimate details set in fantasy lands that exist only in his readers' dreams.

If you'd like to keep up with the world of Solendrea and the extraordinary people and places that exist there, visit: www.solendrea.com.

You can also follow Martin on Twitter and Goodreads. Email inquiries can be addressed to: martin@solendrea.com.